Dedicated to my Cyndi

The Search for Amir

by
James Steele

The Search for Amir

Published byJames Steel April 2024

ISBN: 979-8-218-40847-3

Cover Design and Interior Layout by Alane Pearce
Cover Art: Designed in Canva using AI by Alane Pearce
Contact Alane Pearce, Professional Writing Services, LLC at: *AlanePearceCoaching.com/contact*

Contents

Chapter 1

My dog, Pal, and I walked into my office downstairs from my apartment in a refurbished house on Bomar Street just off Montrose Avenue in Houston. The streets are narrow and in disrepair. It is an old neighborhood that has a mix of mostly colorful older homes, many of which have been fixed up to accommodate the increasingly affluent white-collar workers looking for places near to the offices in downtown Houston. Given the lack of any zoning restrictions in Houston, many also contained offices. I was holding a latte from a Starbucks just around the corner.

Pal, a six-year-old mix between a collie and German shepherd, padded over to my desk where he knew a bag of treats was located. As always, I gave him one. He eyed the bag hopefully for another. "Nope, gotta keep you in shape for all that assistant private eye work you'll be doing." He responded by flopping down at my feet as I sat down at my desk.

It was late May and the heat and humidity that would plague the city until late September was just beginning to set in along the Gulf Coast. I flipped open my MacBook Air to find and delete the usual garbage messages telling me what I need to buy in order to be a high performing private detective. There was also an email from my sister chastising me for not staying in touch with my mom and dad. Unfortunately, there was nothing that sounded like new business for my less than thriving new profession. The good news was that I was my own boss and my prospects for success providing investigative services and security for corporate clients in southeast Texas by most accounts looked positive.

I had spent six great years in the Army until I was wounded in a firefight in Afghanistan that forced me to either transfer from my elite ranger battalion to a unit where I would no longer be on parachute status or leave the Army. I opted for the latter. It was a hard decision. I loved the Army. Being an Army officer was a family tradition. My grandfather had fought in World War II. My father had fought in Vietnam and had been awarded a Silver Star and Purple Heart trying to save a wounded soldier. In a strangely similar scenario, I had received the same awards forty-five years later in Afghanistan. Fortunately, my wounds have healed well, and I am excited about my new career as a gumshoe.

Just as I switched to the online news on my computer, there was a light knock on the door. Before I could even say, "Come in," a tall well-dressed, very attractive woman in her early forties stepped into my office. Her makeup was impeccable. Her shoulder length blonde hair showed the work of an expensive salon. She wasn't quite a ten, but an easy nine.

"Are you John Remington?"

"Yes, how can I help you?" She nodded her head as she carefully set her Hermes Birkin handbag on the edge of my desk and sat down in a chair facing me. When she looked into my eyes, she burst into tears. I sometime have that effect on women. I opened my top desk drawer and handed her a tissue, which she used to blow her nose in a lady-like manner. Then she looked up at me and said, "Does your dog bite?"

"No, not as long as people are nice to me."

She looked up at me and said, "I need your help. Do you have a gun?"

I'm often accused of being a smart ass and my initial thought was to say, "Yeah, and here in Texas so does everyone else." Instead, I said, "Yes, I do, why do you ask?"

"I think someone is going to kill me or my son." Before I could respond, she said,

"I read about you on line. It said you had been an Army Ranger who fought in Iraq and Afghanistan, can you help me?"

"Maybe I can. Why don't you start at the beginning and tell who you are and why you think you and your family are in danger."

Tears welled up again, but she held them back and explained her situation. "My name is Karen Lahoud. It's my husband, Amir. I fear he is mixed up with some very bad people."

I gestured for her to continue.

"Amir came to Houston fifteen years ago from Lebanon. I was born and raised here. We fell in love and were married shortly thereafter. "He is wonderful provider, and we are well off financially. He imports goods from all over the world, especially Mexico. Lately, he has been moody and very secretive. Last night, I overheard a phone conversation with my husband arguing with another person. My husband said that it's just too dangerous. Then he began speaking in Arabic."

I asked, "Do you speak Arabic? Did you hear anything else?"

She said, "No, but later that night two men came to our house. I had already gone to bed when I heard them at the door. I looked out the window. My husband went outside to talk to them. I was able to listen to some of the conversation but could only hear when they raised their voices. They began speaking Arabic again but switched to English when one of men said to speak English or Spanish, not Arabic."

"Why do you think you are in danger?"

"Because at one point, one of the men grabbed my husband by the shirt and said that if he cared about his family, he would arrange the shipment."

"Do you know who these men are?"

"No, I've told you everything I know."

"Please Mr. Remington. I need your help and I can pay. You must promise me that you won't tell my husband."

"Call me John, and yes, I will try to help you as long as you are completely truthful with me. Also, you must agree that if I determine that something illegal is going on, we bring in law enforcement even if it could be a problem for your husband."

She paused, and then said, "Of course, but please, please do what you can to protect him. I really think he is over his head with these people."

I said, "I will. There is some background information that I will need to get started."

She said, "Oh, thank you. When can you start?"

I was tempted to sound important and tell her that I needed to check my schedule, but since I had no other clients at the moment, I said, "Right now."

Over the next hour, I told her about my daily rate plus expenses and got all the information that I thought I needed to begin, including their home address, his office address, their phone numbers, car types and license numbers, working hours, travel habits, and everything else I could think of to get me started. She promised to send me pictures of her husband and her thirteen-year-old son, Thomas. I gave her my card and told her to call me if anything new occurred or she thought of something that she had not told me.

Chapter 2

I spent the rest of the morning researching Amir Lahoud. He was indeed a successful businessman, who owned an export-import company called Lahoud Enterprises with its office in the upscale Galleria area of Houston. The company website was professional but gave little information as to the company's history or client base. There was a picture of Amir. He looked to be in his early fifties. He was a balding man that appeared to be short and somewhat overweight, but it was hard to tell from the picture alone. Further research revealed only that Lahoud Enterprises was privately held and that Amir was the owner with no partners. It was impossible to tell how profitable Lahoud Enterprises was or Amir's net worth. There was nothing on the web to suggest the company or Amir had ever been in trouble or was involved in anything controversial.

I checked the home address that Karen had given me. The Lahoud family lived in River Oaks, the crème de la crème residential area in Houston. That alone suggested that either Amir was doing well financially, or Karen had another source of income. As I researched her background, I found that she indeed came from a wealthy family. Her father, now deceased, had made his fortune in oil. Son Thomas attended St. Barnaby's, a prestigious private school in West Houston.

I called my friend, Captain Bill Fortis, a Houston cop who I had known through my father before I joined the Army. He was once a Marine and had advanced rapidly after joining the police ranks. He had remained in the Marine reserves and had been called up and served in Fallujah during Desert Storm. We have made a habit of having lunch or at least a beer together on a weekly basis.

I asked, "Hey Captain, how are you? You catch any bad guys today?"

"How many times do I have to tell you, Ranger Remington, there are no bad guys? They are simply misunderstood victims of a cruel and intolerant society. I learned that when then made me a police captain. It is not our normal beer night, so you obviously want something."

I said, "Thanks, I'm fine. Well since you mentioned it, there is something. I'm working on a case that has to do with a Lebanese-American businessman, named, Amir Lahoud. His company is called Lahoud Enterprises and is located on Westheimer Avenue. Can you check and see if this guy has anything I should know about?"

"Gosh Ranger, I'm so glad you called. What would I have done today had I not gotten this mission from you? Thank you so much!"

"You're very welcome, and there will an extra donut for you when you get back to me," I said.

"Fuck you very much, Remington."

Fortis called me back in an hour to tell me that Lahoud's extensive criminal record consisted of a speeding ticket he received four years ago and two parking tickets. He said he still wanted the donut with sprinkles.

When in doubt as to what to do next, do something. Pal and I jumped into my Ford 150 pickup, probably the most common vehicle on Texas roads, and drove to the bank to deposit the retainer check I had received from Karen. Then we drove to Amir's office, which was located in two-story building that looked to have about six businesses in occupancy. Based on Karen's description, I found Amir's car, a new white Mercedes 600 sedan, parked in the rear of the building. I pulled into the Dunkin Donut lot next door. Then I began the part that every private investigator loves most, the stake out.

After an hour, the boredom was aggravated by hunger pangs. I went into the donut shop telling myself that I will get something healthy – truly an oxymoron. I returned to the truck with a bag of cinnamon donuts, which I heard were good for you because of the cinnamon, and a large coffee. I hate the taste of coffee, so I put enough milk and sugar in it to mask the taste.

I wondered what PIs had done before they invented cell phones. I used the time to catch up on emails, texts, and calls that I had not returned. I called my sister, who proceeded to once again tell that I needed to call our mom at least once a week. Then she launched into discourse about the problems with the local school system, her husband's preoccupation with golf instead of her, and that her refrigerator had just gone belly up and would cost over three thousand dollars to replace. After twenty minutes without getting a word in edgewise and rolling my eyes repeatedly, I finally interrupted her to say, "Great talking to you, Sis, gotta go, bye."

Four hours later, Amir came out of the office, got into the Mercedes and drove south on Westheimer Road with me in careful pursuit. The traffic was ideal for following someone. It was relatively light, but enough cars to not alert Amir to my presence.

He was apparently not going home, unless he had a really strange short cut. After ten minutes of driving, he pulled into a small shopping center parking lot on Richmond Avenue. I drove past and pulled into the parking lot for a fast-food restaurant next door. I stopped where I could see Amir's car. A minute later, a young, very attractive, dark-haired woman got into his car. I turned to Pal, "The plot thickens." He wagged his tail once. He is a perceptive dog.

Chapter 3

I followed Amir and his dark-haired passenger to a high-rise apartment complex off Beltway 8 on the west side of Houston. They drove into a gated parking garage. I pulled into a visitor spot in front of the building in hopes they would come through the lobby, but they did not. I rolled down the windows in the truck part way for Pal and went into the lobby in time to see the elevator going from the third floor to the sixth. I went back to my truck and waited until a car entered the garage and followed it through the gate. I drove up to see if Amir's car was parked on the third level. It was there next to the entrance to the apartment complex from the parking garage.

Being the clever sleuth that I am, I deduced that she either lived on the sixth floor or they were visiting someone there. I parked in an empty space in the garage near the entry to the apartment complex.

The parking garage only had three levels and I couldn't enter the apartment complex without a card entry, so I acted as though I was checking my truck until someone parked and walked toward the entry. I arrived at the door just after a very large man in shorts and a t-shirt two sizes too small that rode up above a round belly. I followed him into the apartment complex and down a corridor to the elevators. I pushed the sixth floor. The big guy pushed the seventh.

I exited the elevator on the sixth floor. There were eight apartments on the sixth floor, none of which had names posted. I walked back to the elevator as the door to 602 opened and an older man and woman came out and walked toward me. I pushed the down button as they approached. We all exited on the third floor, and they headed to the parking garage. I went back up to the sixth floor and tried to look like I belonged there. Unfortunately, that wasn't easy unless you were a potted plant. After spending the next hour going from the sixth to the third floor and back and seeing no one, I decided to change the plan.

I drove out of the parking garage and parked in the adjacent lot where I could see the cars exiting the garage. While I waited for a new development, I gave Pal some food and water out of my "go bag" that I kept behind the seat of my truck. The "go bag" was a carry-over from Army days. It contained a .45 caliber Glock 21 and several boxes of ammunition for the Glock and the .357 Sig H&K Compact that I carried on my hip. In addition to some food and bottled water, the bag also had a change of clothing, a towel, a shaving kit, toothbrush, first aid kit and gun cleaning gear. I settled back into the stakeout mode.

Boredom set in after an hour, so I called my mother, "Hi Mom. Sorry I haven't called lately. I've been super busy with my new job."

She responded, "John, I hope you're not working for some shyster lawyer following cheating husbands around. That kind of work is below you,"

"No Mom, I'm doing high class investigations." Here I sat waiting for a guy who might well be cheating on his wife.

She said, "John, when are you going to get married? Thanks to your sister, at least I have one grandchild."

"Mom, don't start with that again."

"Well, you're not getting any younger, you know. What are you now, thirty-five?"

"No, Mom, I'm thirty."

"Well, whatever. By the way, what happened to that nice girl you dated last year? What was her name, Ingrid?"

"'Her name was Elaine, Mom. She turned out to be a stalker, kind of like the woman in that movie with Clint Eastwood."

She said, "Oh, John, she wasn't that bad."

"Yes, Mom. She was that bad."

At a brief pause, I said, "Great talking to you, Mom, I really need to go to work now, bye."

The girl that Mom was talking about was Jackie Madison. I met her when I was stationed at Fort Lewis, Washington. My Ranger battalion was home based there, but we were gone most of the time, either in Iraq or Afghanistan. In retrospect, she may have been more infatuated with the fact that I was a Ranger than my good looks and captivating personality. We had a torrid love affair that lasted several months while I was back at Fort Lewis. As the initial infatuation began to wear off, I noticed that she was becoming exceptionally clingy. She insisted I spend every off-duty moment with her. When I took a short leave to see my parents in Texas, she wanted to know everyone I was going to see. She called me at least three times a day. The crowning blow was when she showed up at my parent's home in College Station, Texas unannounced. She told my parents that we were planning to get married soon. I was amazed because I had never discussed marriage and had no intention of doing so with her. I cut my leave short to avoid long explanations. The thing that saved me was that my battalion deployed to Afghanistan. I know I was the happiest soldier in my outfit to deploy.

Two hours later, Amir drove his white Mercedes out of the parking garage. He was alone. I followed him along Westheimer Road. He turned onto River Oaks Boulevard. He pulled into his driveway at his home near the River Oaks Country Club. I waited for a few minutes and left.

I went home. As usual, Pal was glad to be home. His tail was moving like a metronome. I sat at my desk and Pal curled up on the floor next to me. I made a list of what I knew – it was pretty short.

Karen was afraid for herself and her family.

Two men, one who spoke Arabic and another who spoke Spanish, threatened Amir and his family if he failed to make a "shipment."

Amir had a clean record.

Amir's company was privately held and appeared to be doing well.

Karen came from a wealthy family.

Amir had picked up a woman and was with her at an apartment complex off Beltway 8.

Pal and I were sitting in the living room channel surfing the cable news stations when my cell phone rang. I answered, "Hello, it's eleven o'clock, this better be important."

A voice speaking in a whisper said, "John, John Remington, is that you?"

"Yes," I said.

"It's Karen, I need to meet you right now. Something is dreadfully wrong."

Chapter 4

We agreed to meet at a MacDonald's on Memorial Parkway. I arrived first. Ten minutes later, she drove into the parking lot. Like Amir, she had a new Mercedes, but a mere 500 series. This one was silver. I flashed my lights and waved. When she saw me, she drove up and parked next to me. She got out of her car, looked around and then climbed into my truck.

Karen looked good. She was wearing tight jeans, cowboy boots and an expensive crème colored blouse. She looked at me and again broke into tears. As was becoming a routine, I gave her a tissue and she blew her nose. I waited to hear what was new.

Karen finally stopped crying and told me what happened that had caused her to be so upset. She said, "John, Amir came home tonight very upset, but when I asked him what was wrong, he wouldn't talk about it. He said that he was going out of town on business and would be gone for a week or two. When I asked him where he was going, he was evasive. I asked if this had something to do with the men that came to the house last night, he shook his head, went to the bedroom and locked the door. What should I do?"

"Okay, let's take this a step at a time. First, is there any reason that you know of that Amir would pick up a woman on Westheimer and take her to an apartment complex on beltway 8?"

She froze. She acted like I had hit her with a baseball bat. "Of course not, but his office is on Westheimer, maybe he was giving someone a ride home."

I said, "Maybe so. Let's not assume the worst. I'll check it out. In the meantime, see if you can find out where Amir is going and when he is leaving. I also want to know your schedule as well as Thomas's for the next week."

"I take Thomas to school at eight in the morning and pick him up at three. I usually run errands and go to the fitness center during the day," she said.

"Call me if you find out anything about Amir's travel plans. I'll be watching you and Thomas. Try not to worry, it's going to be okay." The phrase *final last words* came to mind.

She put her head on my shoulder and squeezed my arm. "Thank you, John. I'm really scared."

I opened the door and told her we would talk tomorrow and I watched her drive off. Then I drove home thinking that my list just got longer. It was after one o'clock by the time I parked and entered my apartment. I wasn't tired and my mind was racing. Amir's announcement that he was leaving town was a new twist. Was that connected to the men that Karen had seen at their house the previous night? Was there a connection between the dark-haired woman and those men? Maybe the trip had nothing to do with the men at all. There was a good chance that Amir was doing what middle-aged men are known to do – having an affair with a younger woman. Amir was apparently a wealthy guy. That alone might attract women. The truth is that I had no idea what was going on with Amir. Rather than a whole bunch of speculation, I finally decided that I needed more information about Amir's business. I decided to talk it over with Karen in the morning.

Pal had already settled in at the foot of my bed for the night and showed little interest in my problem. In fact, he looked at me as if to say, "Why the hell don't you turn out the light and go to sleep." So I did.

Chapter 5

I got up at five o'clock and put on my workout clothes. I let Pal out in the back yard and fed him. Then I went to my gym that was a short three blocks away. I decided to put Amir and Karen out of my mind for a couple of hours. After sixty minutes on the weights, I came home to find my landlady, Mary Fitzgerald, giving instructions to several Latino workers trimming a little gem magnolia in the front yard.

"Top of morning to ya, Miss Mary," I said in my best Irish brogue.

In a similarly phony Irish accent, she responded, "John, yer a sight fer sore eyes, ya are! And how is my favorite mutt, Pal?"

"Pal's fine, he asked if he could spend some time with you today rather than riding around with me."

"Tell him to come and see me anytime."

I took a quick shower, ate some Greek yogurt and drank one of those bottled Starbucks coffee drinks that are so good because they taste nothing like coffee. The morning traffic was heavy, but I managed to arrive at the Lahoud home by 7:40.

I decided to park down the street and wait. At 7:50, the garage door opened, and Karen's car backed out. I could see that Thomas was with her. They turned toward me. I went around the block and fell in behind them at a light at the access road to I-610, the ring road around Houston. As we got closer to St, Barnaby's, I noticed a black SUV behind me. I slowed and pulled to the curb. The SUV drove by. There were two men in it. They paid no attention to me. I fell in behind the SUV.

It was a short drive to St. Barnaby's. The black SUV pulled to the curb as Karen stopped to drop Thomas off at the school. As she pulled away, the SUV pulled forward and the driver honked the horn. Thomas looked back as the man in the passenger seat waived and held up what looked like a book. He said something to Thomas that I couldn't hear. Thomas started to walk back towards the SUV. Traffic was blocking my way as more parents were stopping to drop off their kids. I jumped from the truck and ran towards Thomas who was some twenty yards from the SUV. I called to Thomas, "Don't go over there." The men in the SUV must have heard me or seen me running toward them and immediately pulled away. By the time I had reached where the SUV had been, Thomas had gone into the school. I repeated the license number several times in my mind as I returned to the truck. I wrote it down and called Captain Fortis.

"Hey Cap, what's happening?"

"Well Ranger Remington, it's been a whole day since you've asked me for something, the PI business must be slow. I truly live for these calls," he said.

"I feel the love. Listen, this case has just taken on a new twist. I think someone may have tried to kidnap my client's kid."

"What does 'may have tried' mean, did it happen or not?"

"Well, I thought it was going to happen, so I jumped in, and the bad guys took off," I said.

"Are you sure they were trying to kidnap the kid?"

"Pretty sure," I said knowing where this was going.

"Shall I call out the SWAT team now? Better yet, let's get the National Guard and the Texas Rangers."

"Can you at least just run a plate for me?"

"Why didn't you just ask?"

I gave him the plate number and the make and color of the SUV. He promised to "stop everything the HPD was doing" to address my needs.

Next, I called Karen and told her what had happen at the school. Her reaction was predictable. She freaked out. "Oh my God! Is Thomas okay?"

"Karen, Thomas is fine. "

"Should I go pick him up?"

"If it will make you feel better, call the school and tell them to make sure no one but you can pick him up."

I told her it was time to confront Amir and suggested we all meet right away. Karen said Amir had left her a note saying he was leaving and would call her in a few days. He didn't say where he was going. She said he was gone when she got up at six, so he must have left very early. I told her that now I was concerned for her safety as well as that of Thomas and asked if she and Thomas could go somewhere away from Houston for a while. She told me that Thomas was finishing his exams today and would be out for the summer. She said they had talked about a visit to Dallas to see her sister. I told her to pack their bags, lock the doors, and wait at the house until I got there.

As I was pulling into their driveway, my cell phone rang. It was Captain Fortis. "Well Ace Ventura, I ran your plate. Either you forgot the number, or the black SUV was really a red Chevy truck. Actually, neither is right. We contacted the owner of the truck, who went out to check. He confirmed that his front plate was missing. Looks like a dead end."

"Thanks, Captain. It also confirms that they were trying to kidnap the kid. I'll get back to you when I have something more definitive."

Chapter 6

Karen opened the door before I rang the bell. She had several large and expensive Louis Vuitton suitcases lined up by the door. She had wasted no time getting ready to leave.

"Karen, what I am going to tell you is very important. Do not tell anyone where you are going. Keep your phone fully charged so I can talk to you day or night. Now, write down your sister's address and phone number for me."

She did as I had asked and said, "What about Amir? He is obviously in great danger. I have no idea where he is going or why."

"Let's see what we can find out. Call his office and ask if they know where Amir is going. Does he have an assistant or secretary?"

She replied, "He has an office manager, a bookkeeper, and a business assistant. Who should I call?"

"Let's start with the office manager. Try to make the call routine and non-threatening."

She dialed the office on speaker. A woman answered, "Lahoud Enterprises, may I help you?"

"Hi Kirsten, it's Karen. How are you?"

"I'm fine. It's good to hear your voice. If you are calling for Amir, he's not in the office."

"I know, he left in a rush this morning and forgot to tell me what hotel he'll be at. Do you know?"

"Gosh, Karen, I have no idea. I didn't even know he was leaving until I played his voice message at the office this morning. He said he would be gone the rest of the week and to cancel the rest of his appointments. Everyone here is in the dark."

"Thanks, Kirsten. Please call me if you hear from him."

"Okay, that was well done, but another dead end," I said. "Let's try plan B. Does Amir have a home office?"

"Yes, follow me."

We spent the next two hours going through Amir's desk, cabinets and closet. His computer was locked, and Karen did not know the password. I tried the usual ones, like "password," his name, her name, number sequences, his birthday, their anniversary, no luck.

"Think, Karen. What would Amir use for a password? Do you have his bank card number?"

"No, I don't know anything, John. What are we going to do?"

"Relax, what are his hobbies?"

He's kind of a car nut and he likes to play golf," she said, "That is what he does when he's not working."

"Okay, let's start with cars, what are his favorites?"

She said, "Oh, I don't know. Mercedes and Ferraris, I guess."

I tried every model I could think of, but nothing worked.

"Okay, how about golf? Who is his favorite golfer?"

"He was a big Tiger Woods fan for a while."

I tried every variation of Tiger Woods to no avail.

It was time to pick up Thomas and I did not want to be late. We arrived at 2:45 and were first in line to pick him up. There was no sign of the black SUV or any other suspicious vehicle.

Thomas came out at 3:05 and climbed into the back seat. He was bubbling with enthusiasm over something. "I aced every test except biology, but I think I did okay on that one too."

Then he noticed me. Karen introduced us and we shook hands.

"You're the guy I saw running toward me this morning, what was up with that?"

Karen told him I was a private investigator she had hired to protect the family. That triggered a barrage of questions from Thomas.

"Are you packing?"

"Yes."

"Can I see it?"

"No."

"What kind is it, a revolver or an automatic?

"Automatic."

"What kind?"

"H&K, 357 sig."

"Cool, did you ever shoot anybody?"

I said, "Enough questions."

Thank heavens we had arrived at the house. Karen told Thomas about the trip to Dallas but told him he couldn't tell anyone. As we loaded the car, Karen asked Thomas if he knew his dad's password. He said that he did not. I asked Thomas, "Do you play golf with your dad?"

"Sure, we play almost every weekend. My goal is to beat my dad."

"Who's his favorite pro?"

"That's easy, McIlroy, hands down."

I went back to the computer and typed in McIlroy, upper case, and lower case. Nothing. Then I tried "Rory." Bingo! The screen came to life. The last message received was a flight confirmation today from Brownsville to Houston followed by a second flight to Paris that left thirty minutes ago and then a third flight to Beirut. There was also a hotel confirmation at the Hilton on Charles de Gaulle Street in Beirut. What the hell was going on?

Karen was hovering over me as I copied the flight and hotel information into my iphone.

"What should we do now, John? Can you find Amir?"

I thought about the alternatives. I could wait and see what happened. Maybe Amir would call Karen. Maybe I could talk to Amir by phone when he got to Beirut. Amir's Middle East trip made me wonder what the "shipment" was all about. I also kept thinking about the dark-haired woman that Amir picked up after work yesterday.

"Okay, Karen, I'll follow Amir, but this is going to get expensive. Are you okay with that?"

"Yes, yes, oh, thank you, John. Please find Amir and get him out of this mess."

"I will be on the first flight tomorrow. There are a few things I want to check on before I leave."

I followed Karen and Thomas to the 610 Loop and then north on I-45 to be sure no one was following them to Dallas. Karen was a careful driver. Unlike me, she drove exactly the speed limit. I followed along patiently. On the north side of Conroe, I turned around and drove home.

I thought about what I was getting myself into. This mission was beginning to get interesting.

Chapter 7

I spent the evening preparing for my trip to Lebanon. I had never been there before, so I did some serious research on the country. To put it bluntly, the place was in turmoil. The U.S. State Department recommended against traveling there. It was a shame. I recall Beirut once being referred to as the Paris of the Middle East. It was once a model of how Muslims and Christians could live together peacefully.

I went to Mary's apartment to let her know that I was leaving and to ask her to take care of Pal while I was gone. As always, she was happy to keep Pal. She loved him as much as I did. I always knew he would be in good hands with her. She asked me where I was going.

"I'll be in Beirut for a few days on business."

She threw her hands up and said, "John. Have you lost your mind? I read the papers and watch the news. They are killing one another over there. Please don't go."

"Sorry, Mary, but I have to go."

"Please be careful. I'm going to ask Father Malloy to say a mass for you to keep you safe."

"Thank you, Mary."

She made a wonderful Texas dinner of chicken fried steak with mashed potatoes, white gravy and black-eyed peas. I could feel my arteries clogging with every scrumptious bite. Pal gave me his most mournful look, the one that pretended that he had not been fed for a week. I finally caved in and went into the closet where Mary kept dog treats and gave him one. He swallowed it and looked at me hopefully. "Okay, Pal, here's one more and that's all."

In a few minutes, he gave me the look again. This time I was tough and only gave him one more treat. After eating a piece of Mary's pecan pie, I declared nirvana, thanked her, and waddled up to my apartment. Pal followed closely behind. He didn't waddle.

In the morning, I went to the small shopping center where Amir picked up the dark-haired woman. There were fifteen small businesses in the center. I went into all of the shops and asked about the dark-haired woman. No one remembered her. It was another dead end.

I decided to go to the apartment complex where Amir took the woman yesterday. This time I parked in a visitor spot in front of the building. Off the lobby, there was an office that was marked "Rental Management." There was a small woman in her fifties sitting behind a polished wooden desk. There was a nameplate that read, "Harriet Stone." She was wearing a dark skirt and pink blouse with a small cross on a gold chain around her neck. Her gray hair was pulled back in a tight bun. She wore gold-rimmed glasses half way down her rather long nose. She looked up over the glasses and asked, "May I help you?"

I flashed my best smile and said, "I'm investigating a missing person and need your help. Have you seen this man?" I showed her a picture of Amir.

"No, I'm sorry. I don't recall ever seeing this person. Who is he?"

"His name is Amir Lahoud. He has been missing for several days. He was seen entering an apartment on the sixth floor of this complex two days ago with a dark-haired woman. Would it be possible to have a list of occupants on that floor?"

"I'm sorry, sir, but I can't give out that information without the approval of the occupants. Are you a policeman?"

I showed her my license and said, "I'm a private investigator, hired by Mrs. Lahoud. She and her son are very worried about Amir and fear foul play."

"Oh my, I don't know. This is quite irregular. I will have to check with Mr. Roberts the building manager. He will be back this afternoon."

"Harriet, time is critical when dealing with a missing person. His family would be very grateful for your help," I said.

I showed her a picture of the smiling family that Karen had sent to my phone. I could sense some empathy developing. She tapped a key on her computer, which was facing her. I couldn't see the screen. "What floor did you say that he was seen on?"

"The sixth floor," I said.

She tapped the keyboard again and appeared to scroll down.

"Mr. Remington, I'm going to have a cup of coffee, would you like me to bring you one?"

"That would be terrific. Thank you."

She left the room. I swiveled the screen and saw the list of occupants on the sixth floor. It had to be my charming smile. I took out my phone and photographed the screen. When I checked the picture, the names and contact information were clear and readable. I swiveled the screen back into its original position.

Five minutes later, she returned with two cups of coffee. I thanked her, and said I owed her a lunch. She beamed.

The list of occupants did not reveal anything at first blush. I did notice that either a male name or couples occupied 601, 603, 604, 605 and 606. There was none that suggested a woman was the only resident.

As I left the apartment complex, my cell phone rang. It was Karen. She confirmed that she had arrived at her sister's home without incident. She said, "Amir just called me. He said he had tried to call the house and had gotten no answer. He was very concerned when I told him what had happened with Thomas at school. He said I should take a trip to visit my sister now that Thomas was finished with school for the summer."

I said, "Did he tell you where he was?"

She responded, "He only said he was traveling to several different locations and would call in a few days, but not to worry."

"Did you let on that you knew he was going to Lebanon?"

She said, "No, it was a very short conversation. He talked to Thomas briefly then cut it short saying his plane was about to leave."

I read the list of occupants, including 602, to see if she recognized any of the names. She did not. I told her I was leaving in a few hours and would be in touch when I arrived in Beirut.

I thought about what Karen had just told me. Amir had been vague about where he was. Why had he called now? Maybe he was just touching base. That would be normal. What wasn't normal was not telling Karen where he was and where he was going.

I also couldn't be sure that the dark-haired woman was even related to the threat to Amir and his family or to the "dangerous shipment." Maybe Amir was having an affair with the dark-haired woman. I couldn't allow myself to get preoccupied with her now that Amir had left for Lebanon, which seemed directly related to the threat and what I had been hired to prevent.

Although I had the nagging suspicion that she was part of the equation, I decided to put the dark-haired woman on hold and focus on finding Amir.

Then there was the issue of a possible kidnapping of Thomas. That alone should have prompted Amir to come straight home. Why didn't he do that? Maybe Karen didn't describe it as a real kidnapping attempt.

I was about to leave for the airport when my cell phone rang again. When I answered, Karen said, "My sister just came home and said she thought there was someone watching the house. John, I'm scared. What should I do?"

"Tell me exactly what your sister saw."

Karen said, "My sister said that there were two men in a car parked down the street. She said they ducked down when she drove by. Normally, she wouldn't pay much attention, but because of what I had told her about why I was there, she was being extra vigilant."

I said, "Karen, have your sister call the police and tell them you think that someone is watching your house. I don't want to take any chances. I'm going to delay my trip to Lebanon and come to Dallas. I want you to text me your sister's address. Most important of all, I want you and Thomas to stay in the house and lock all of the doors and windows. I'll be there in a few hours.

I had my bag already packed, so all I had to do was grab my H&K and my Glock 21. My go bag was already in the truck. I climbed in and headed for Dallas. I told myself that being flexible was an important part of the job.

Chapter 8

I drove north on the Hardy toll road to The Woodlands. The afternoon traffic in Houston was heavy initially but thinned out after I got to Conroe on I-45. I turned on my radar detector and set the cruise control on ninety. I had to slow down just before arriving in Huntsville when the radar detector started beeping. There was a speed trap set up as I crested a hill. I drove by the state trooper at exactly 65 miles an hour – the posted speed limit.

I arrived at Karen's sister's house in just under four hours. I pulled into the driveway and went up to the door. Karen opened the door and greeted me with a hug. Thomas also was glad to see me. Karen introduced me to her sister, Joan, who was a single mom with a four-year-old daughter. We sat in her small living room. Joan asked if I would like some lemonade. I said, "Thanks, that would be terrific."

Joan brought me a tall glass of lemonade and I asked what had happened since we spoke a few hours earlier.

"After our call, Joan called the police and reported the two men that were watching the house. About thirty minutes later, an officer came to the door. He said he was investigating the report. Joan described the car as a black SUV with two men inside. As I told you, she said they ducked out of sight as she approached."

"Did she get a license number?" I asked.

"No, the policeman asked her the same question. She said that she thought about going around the block but thought that would alert them. He asked her exactly where the car was parked. She told him."

"What happened after that?"

Karen said, "The policeman left. He came back in about twenty minutes and told us that the car was gone, but that one of her neighbors had seen it as well. He said to call if the car came back."

I said, "Karen, I hate to tell you this, but I think you need to go somewhere else. Is there a place that you and Thomas would like to go? It would be best if your sister went with you."

Karen said, "We could go to a spa I know in Hot Springs, Arkansas. It's not so far to drive."

Joan said, "Let's go, that will be fun."

I said, "Okay, sounds like a plan. It's getting late. You both get packed up so you can leave first thing in the morning. I'm going to check around the house."

I went out and got in the truck. I drove all around the neighborhood. There was no sign of the black SUV. I pulled back into driveway and walked around the house. It was not the most secure place I had ever seen. There was a sliding glass door in the rear that was the most likely avenue of approach for someone trying to break into the house. I decided that I would stay near that rear door throughout the night.

Karen, Joan and the kids watched TV until ten o'clock. They all went to bed. I checked all the doors and windows again and lay down on a couch near the sliding door. It was a very quiet neighborhood. The streetlights were spaced far apart. I figured that if something were going to happen, it would be well after midnight. I decided to sleep until midnight. I set my watch to wake me up.

My watched buzzed at midnight. I shut it off and walked through the house checking the windows and doors. I looked out the front windows. Everything was quiet. I sat back down on the couch. I had both the H&K and the Glock 21 next to me.

At three o'clock, I thought I heard a noise. It sounded like a rustle, which would have been normal, but there was no wind. I got up quietly and looked out the sliding door. There was nothing amiss. I moved slowly to the front window and looked up and down the street. The black SUV was parked on the street about twenty yards from the front of the house.

I decided not to wake up the others. Instead, I went back and positioned myself next to the sliding door. I could see along the house to only one side, but it was the side where the SUV was parked. I waited. Several minutes passed before I saw a shadow moving along the wall of the house.

He approached the sliding door very quietly. He was a large man. He tried the sliding door. It was locked. He slid something into the latch, and it clicked. I watched as he opened the sliding door and stepped inside. He had an automatic pistol in his right hand.

We were no more than five feet apart when I said, "Drop the weapon or you're dead."

I startled him and his reaction was immediate. Instead of doing the logical thing, he fired before he aimed. The bullet stung my left shoulder. Almost simultaneously, I fired back, two shots center of mass from the Glock 21. The forty-five slugs put him down hard. He managed to fire one more shot as he was going down, but it went into the ceiling. I flipped on the white light mounted on the Glock, picked up his pistol and knelt next to him. He was in bad shape and no longer a threat. Now I was worried about his partner in the black SUV. I went to the front window just in time to see the SUV drive off fast. I grabbed a dishtowel and tried to stop his bleeding, although it looked useless. One of the bullets had hit him in the heart or very close. The other was in the center of his chest. I asked him who sent him, but he was gone.

Karen was the first to come out. I told her to keep the kids in the bedroom and that everything was okay. I picked up the phone in the kitchen and called 911. I told them that I had just shot an armed intruder. I gave my name and the address of the house.

I put my H&K in my bag and the Glock on the kitchen table. The police and ambulance arrived within about five minutes. The uniformed cops handcuffed me and the EMTs bandaged my shoulder. They said I should go to the hospital and have it stitched up. There was no serious damage. Karen and Joan objected to me being handcuffed, but I told them that the cops were following normal procedures. I said I wanted to wait for the detectives before I went to the hospital.

About thirty minutes later, a detective named Higgins showed up. He was an impressive looking black cop. I guessed him to be early forties. He looked like he could have been a wide receiver for the Cowboys in his younger days. He was a little taller than me. I would guess six two, well built with no fat. He wore pressed jeans and a polo shirt under a sport coat that concealed his sidearm.

He interviewed Karen and Joan first. Then he sat down with me. He checked my license for the handgun and my personal protection officer card. The forensic team arrived and started collecting evidence. I knew it was going to be an ordeal.

I gave Higgins all the details starting with what had occurred back in Houston and ending with the two shots into the intruder.

He asked if anyone could vouch for me in Houston. I gave him Captain Fortis's name. He said, "Write out your statement and just keep it to what happened here in the house. Everybody's consistent here. This was a clear case of self-defense – a no brainer."

I said, "There is a lot more to this than an intruder breaking into a house. This may have been another attempt to kidnap Thomas or his mother. I'd appreciate a call when you ID this guy. It might lead us to the mastermind. I suspect that this guy was a low life at the bottom of the food chain."

Higgins said, "Okay, make sure I have a good number for you. I'm sure we'll have more questions down the road."

I said, "These guys don't give up. The uniform that responded to the call from Joan earlier talked to the neighbors. He may have something."

Higgins replied, "I've already put a call into him."

"I figured you had. I've told Joan and Karen to get the hell out of here until things settle down."

He said, "Yeah, they told me they planned to hang out in Hot Springs. I told them that I thought that was a good idea. We're going to keep a close eye on the house just in case they come back for a look see. Also, I'll need your weapon for the ballistics. I'm sure you've got another one."

I said, "True enough, no problem."

By the time we finished, it was mid-morning. Karen, Joan and the kids were all packed up and ready to go. Just as I had done in Houston, I followed them for about ten miles to be sure they weren't being followed. When I was sure, I turned around and headed south on I-45 to Houston.

I stopped at one of 24-hour emergency centers along the freeway that had become popular lately. This one advertised a wait time of six minutes on the lighted sign in the front of the building. I went in and told the person at the desk that I thought

I needed some stitches in my arm. She asked for my driver's license and my insurance card. I gave her those. I was waiting for her to ask me how the injury happened, but she just said, "Okay John, please have a seat and someone will be with you shortly."

I thanked her and sat down in front of the TV mounted on the wall. When the commercial ended, there was an attractive reporter standing in front of Joan's house. The caption said, "Shooting in quiet neighborhood - intruder dead." She was interviewing a neighbor who was saying, "I can't believe it. Nothing like this has ever happened on our street. That lady lives there with her little daughter. They are the nicest people. I'm so glad they are okay.

The camera switched to a neighbor, a heavyset fellow wearing a baseball cap. He said, "These are good folks here, but we don't put up with people breaking in. I'm sure glad I live in Texas where you can have a gun to defend yourself. Thank God for the Second Amendment."

Just as he finished his comments, an attractive woman in scrubs came in and said, "John Remington."

I waived and said, "That's me."

She said, "I'm Veronica Zamora. I'm a PA. Come on back and let's take a look at that arm."

She unwrapped the bandage that the EMT had put on my arm. The wound was not very deep, but it was still oozing blood. She looked at it closely and announced, "Doesn't look too bad. What happened?"

She had asked THE question. I knew if I told her that I had been shot, I would be there for hours. She would have to notify the police, fill out reports, ugh. So I said, "Stupid me, I was helping with a home repair and a nail gun went off and grazed me."

Her brow wrinkled as she examined the wound. She said, "You're lucky. Those things are dangerous. Most accidents with them are from someone shooting their hand or their foot."

I wanted to say that it was the best thing I could come up with on such short notice. I just played dumb and smiled. That usually caused women to swoon. In this case, it didn't work. She cleaned the wound with alcohol, which stung. I didn't let on that I felt a thing. She used five stitches to close the wound. She bandaged it up again. She asked me when the last time was I had had a tetanus shot. I knew the exact date because it was the day I was wounded in Afghanistan. I said, "Thirteen months ago."

She said, "I'm giving you another one just to be safe."

I thanked her. As I walked out she said, "Nail gun, right?"

When I got back in the truck, I recapped in my mind everything that had happened in the past forty-eight hours. How did all of these events tie together? First, there was the "dangerous shipment" and the guy who met with Amir at his house that spoke Arabic. Was that coincidental? It definitely was not. Amir's hotel reservation in Beirut proved that. Then there was the infamous "dark haired woman." How did she tie in? Maybe she didn't at all. Maybe she was having an unrelated affair with Amir. Last, but not least, there was the kidnapping attempt at Thomas's school and the shootout at Joan's house. The logical conclusion was that the kidnapping was designed to keep Amir in line and execute the "dangerous shipment" plan.

After four hours of pondering all of these events, I concluded that I really had no idea what was going on. The only thing that made sense was to continue with my previous plan.

I called Karen in her car and told her that unless she objected, I planned to go to Beirut and continue the search for Amir.

She said, "John, please, please find Amir. I'm sure the men that came last night were trying to kidnap Thomas again as a way of getting Amir to help them. Don't you agree?"

"I do agree." I said. I've been thinking about last night and how these guys knew where you and Thomas were. Did you actually tell Amir that you were at Joan's house?"

She said, "Yes, I think we did. He suggested that I go there and when Thomas was talking to him, I think he said we were there. You don't think that Amir was in on the kidnapping of his own son, do you."

I responded, "No, but he might have been under duress, or someone was listening to the conversation. In any case, under no circumstances should you, Thomas, or Joan tell anyone where you are."

"I promise."

Just as I finished the call with Karen, my cell rang. It was Captain Fortis. He said, "What the fuck have you done now and where are you?"

I replied, "Oh, I'm just fine. Thanks for asking. How are you?"

"Don't be a smart ass. I just spent the last twenty minutes on the phone with a detective from DPD lying about what a good guy you are."

I said, "That would be Detective Higgins, a very impressive guy. I gave him your name as a character witness."

"Yeah, I know. Ranger Remington, you are becoming my worst nightmare. I don't even want to answer my phone because I know it's probably about you."

"But you love me, right?" I said.

"All kidding aside, tell me what happened and if it is connected with the kidnapping and the incident in Zippy's parking lot,"

I responded, "I'm not sure, but I think this is all tied to Amir and his trip to Lebanon. I think that these are the same two that tried to kidnap Thomas at the school. It looked like the same black SUV.

He said, "Well that doesn't explain why these guys were in Dallas. How did they know Thomas was in Dallas?"

"Those are great questions.

"That is why I am a police captain."

"Right. I've been asking myself the same one ever since it happened. My supposition is that they want to hold Thomas as a hostage to make sure Amir doesn't back out of the shipment deal. I'm not sure how they knew where he was, but I think that either Karen or Thomas may have let it slip when Amir called them yesterday."

"Makes senses if you think Amir was in on the kidnapping or if the bad guys were listening in on the call," he said. "What's your plan now?"

"Since I can't figure any of this out, I'm going with my original plan. I'm going to Beirut. That is where Amir is supposed to be. His wife wants me to find him and bring him home."

Fortis said, "Well the good news about that is that at least you won't be creating any more work for me here in Houston."

"Don't be too sure, I'm driving back there right now to catch the next flight to Doha and on to Beirut."

"Mother of God, please don't shoot anybody before you get on the plane."

His final words were, "Be safe."

Chapter 9

I stopped by the house to take a shower and let Mary know that I had been delayed but was still going to Beirut. Pal greeted me like I had been gone for a month. He followed me around the apartment. He sat outside the shower until I finished.

Mary insisted that I have something to eat before I headed to the airport. She prepared a turkey sandwich that could have fed three people. I ate every bite. I hadn't realized how hungry I was. It was the first thing I had eaten since last evening.

Pal eyed my turkey sandwich. Then he put his head on my leg and really gave me the look. I said, "No people food for you."

He was not deterred. I asked Mary, "Have you been giving Pal people food, my dear?"

She said, "No, well maybe a snack occasionally when he gets really hungry, or I run out of dog treats. Look at those eyes. How can you say no?"

"There are two bags of dog treats in my pantry. I'll leave them with you before I leave."

I said goodbye to Mary and Pal. They both walked out to the truck with me. Mary waived as I pulled out. Pal had the look that said, "*Where are you going now and who's going to take me for a run in the morning.*" A dog is truly man's best friend.

I arrived at Bush Intercontinental Airport with only a carry-on bag and my passport. Unlike Karen's bag, mine was not a Louis Vuitton. I felt naked without a weapon, especially given where I was going.

It was going to take me twenty-four hours to get to Beirut. After clearing security, I went to the Qatar Airlines lounge in Terminal D. It was quite nice. There was a fully stocked bar and a large array of hot and cold snacks. I wouldn't say I gorged myself but I had a glass of red wine and had a taste of everything. The wine was purely medicinal. I was told that something called resveratrol was good for my heart. It was an excellent excuse in any case.

We boarded the flight forty minutes before the takeoff time. I was in the business class cabin. I decided that this was not bad. We took off right on time. I slept much of the way to Doha, although I didn't miss any meals.

We landed at Hamad International Airport in Doha right on time. I wandered around and marveled at the architecture. What a spectacular facility it is. Changing planes in Doha went smoothly. It was early morning when I arrived at Rafic Hariri International Airport in Beirut. I changed $800 into Lebanese pounds. Fortunately, the Hilton's car that I had arranged before leaving Houston was waiting when I cleared customs.

Driving into the city was a surprise to me. It is a bustling city. It took about twenty minutes on a modern highway to get to the hotel, which Ahmed referred to as Habtoor Grand. I checked in and was given a room on the tenth floor. I went over to the concierge desk and arranged for a car to be on standby. I grabbed my bag and went straight to my room.

When I settled into my room, I tried to formulate a plan. The only thing that made any sense was to make contact with Amir and convince him that I was there to help him keep his family alive and not go to jail himself. I called the front desk and asked to ring his room. He answered on the first ring, and I immediately hung up. Now I knew that he was at the hotel.

Chapter 10

I went down to the lobby and found a comfortable chair where I could observe the elevators. After two hours, Amir finally came out of the elevator with none other than the dark-haired woman that he had picked up in Houston. I followed them into the restaurant for lunch. There was a large buffet with lots of guests. That made it easy for me to sit by their table without raising suspicions. Unfortunately, they were speaking Arabic. Soon two other men joined them. Although they all appeared to be Middle Eastern and were similar in appearance to Amir, one of the men apparently did not speak Arabic and the conversation changed to English. I observed the body language of each of them. Amir was docile. He appeared to be intimidated. If there was an affair ongoing between Amir and the dark-haired woman, it was not apparent even before the two men arrived. The two men were clearly in charge. They pointed their finger at Amir repeatedly as if giving him orders. He nodded each time. I strained to hear what was being said. As I walked by to refill my plate, I heard one of the men say in an accent that sounded Spanish, "Then it's Mexico City tomorrow, no delays."

I had no idea what was going on, but it was obvious that there was a direct link between the dark-haired woman and Amir's travel. It also seemed logical to assume that all were likely involved in the shipment that Karen overheard Amir and the men in Houston discussing.

The group finished lunch and headed for the lobby. I went to the concierge's desk, and they directed me to the car that I had arranged. It was an old black Mercedes with a talkative driver named Ahmed. His English was quite good, and he was anxious to show it off.

"Where we going Mister Remington?"

"Please call me John," I said.

"Okay, Mister John, where to?"

It sounded trite, but the group, including Amir, had gotten into a Lexus, so I said, "Follow that car."

The Lexus turned right on Charles de Gaulle Street and through a circle to Rue Eleven. We turned off Rue Eleven and traveled through a series of narrow streets. I told Ahmed to keep his distance because I didn't want them to know we were following them. He beamed and said, "This is like the American police shows on the television, no?"

"Yes, Ahmed, just like that."

After about fifteen minutes, the Lexus stopped and Ahmed slowed down. He turned to me and said, "This is not a good neighborhood for you, Mister John."

I said, "What do you mean?"

"This area is controlled by Hezbollah's Jihad Council. They often set up checkpoints and it would not be wise for you to be taken by these people, Mister John."

Just as he spoke, four men armed with AK47s came out of a building nearby. I made eye contact with one of the men, who I am sure recognized me as a foreigner. Ahmed had already started turning around when they yelled something in Arabic. Ahmed jammed the accelerator and the car lurched forward.

"Get down, Mister John, get down!"

Just as I did, I heard the familiar popping of the AK on full automatic and the rear window of the car shattered. I felt incredibly helpless with no weapon. Ahmed made a quick turn at the next corner and kept going fast.

"Ahmed, are you okay?"

"*Na'am*, yes, I am fine, Mister John. We were very lucky."

"Lucky, hell, Ahmed. You saved my life. You are a brave man!"

"I saved mine too!" Ahmed said.

We returned to the hotel. I asked Ahmed how much it would cost to fix the window.

"Do not worry, Mister John. Allah will provide."

I put the whole $800 worth of Lebanese pounds in his jacket pocket when we shook hands. It reinforced my belief that there are indeed good people everywhere.

Chapter 11

I was in a quandary. I recalled the first standing order from the old Ranger manual dating back to the 1700s, "Don't forget anything." What was I missing or forgetting? None of it seemed to make much sense, except that this mission had almost gotten Ahmed and me killed. I wasn't sure if Amir was a good guy or a bad guy. Karen's account of the meeting that Amir had with the two men and the reference to the "dangerous shipment" certainly did suggest illegal activity. On the other hand, it could have merely been a term to describe a risky business venture. Even the incident at Thomas' school may have fallen short of a real kidnap attempt, although the stolen license plate and the shootout in Dallas confirmed that it was a real attempt. I couldn't attribute the shooting here in Beirut to Amir and his friends, although their entry into a Hezbollah area was troubling as well. There was lots of smoke, but no fire yet.

So, when in doubt, do something. I called Amir's room. There was no answer. I left a message, "Amir, I am a friend. Meet me in the restaurant at 7PM, please come alone." I felt like I was in a James Bond movie.

I went to the restaurant at 6:30 and waited. By eight o'clock, it was clear that Amir was not coming. I went to the front desk and asked them to ring his room. I was told that he had checked out. What now?

I called the US Embassy and asked for the Army attaché's office. On the first ring, a voice answered, "Major Williamson."

"This is John Remington; I am a private investigator from Houston and need some help. Frankly, I'm not sure where to start, but since I'm ex-Army, I called you."

"Well, we don't get many private eyes around here. What do you need and I'll see if I can help you. When did you serve?"

"I spent most of my ten years in Ranger units. I served in Iraq and more recently in Afghanistan where I took a couple of AK rounds in the legs. That effectively ended my airborne career. I'm here looking for an American citizen that came to Beirut a couple of days ago under strange circumstances. I found him today at the Hilton and when I followed him, my car was shot up. Now he's gone."

"It sounds a bit outside my lane but let me try to help. Where are you now?"

"I'm at the Hilton."

"Have you eaten?"

"No."

"Me neither, I'll see you in the lobby in twenty minutes."

"Great, thanks."

Twenty minutes later on the nose, a tall slender, fit man in his mid to late thirties walked into the hotel. He was wearing black jeans, a tan shirt and a blue sport coat. The bulge over his right hip suggested he was armed.

I walked up to him, "Major Williamson?"

He nodded, "You must be John Remington."

We shook hands and headed for the restaurant. In Arabic, he spoke to the hostess. She led us to a table near the rear of the restaurant. Williamson sat with his back to the wall. His presence gave me a sense of well-being that I hadn't felt since I arrived in Beirut.

He began the conversation, "John, tell me more about yourself. I take it you were infantry?"

"Yes sir, I was commanding a ranger company out of Fort Lewis when I was hit. I loved the Army, but you play the hand you're dealt. One of the rounds did a job on my knee. Actually, I was pretty lucky overall. I spent almost two years in Iraq as well. How about you, Major?"

"First, call me Tom. I'm infantry as well. I'm also a Middle East FAO (Foreign Area Officer), which explains my assignment as the Assistant Army Attaché here in Lebanon. Like you, I fought in Iraq. The Army sent me to Michigan to get a master's degree in Middle Eastern Studies. I've been assigned to the Embassy here for about a year. It's a pretty cool assignment, especially given what is happening in the region. As you know, being a company commander is probably the best job in the Army. I commanded a company in the 82nd Airborne. As a major, you don't command shit. So this is a good time to have an assignment like this one. I'll return to troops next year. Hopefully, I'll get picked up early for lieutenant colonel and get a battalion command. Enough about me tell me what's going on with you?"

I told him the whole story, including the shooting that had occurred that afternoon.

He said, "You were pretty lucky, that driver either saved your life or a whole lot of grief as a hostage. There are places in this city where you definitely shouldn't go." Tom tented his fingers and said, "This shipment thing bothers me. Any idea what it might be?"

"None, but I am assuming a link between here and Mexico. Maybe they intend to smuggle it into the U.S. over the Texas border. The fact that Amir went to Brownsville and flew to Houston and on to Beirut suggests that there is some connection," I said.

"There are more and more indicators that the bad guys are going to go after targets in the U.S." Tom said. "There are definitely sleeper cells there, but they need sophisticated gear. They can easily get rifles and handguns in the U.S., but if they want to make a big splash, they need help from outside."

"That is a pretty scary prospect, Tom. In any case, our interests are aligned. I need to find Amir. You need to find out about the shipment. If we find Amir, we're part way there."

"Give me Amir's full name and address. Do you have a picture?"

I gave him one of the pictures I had gotten from Karen of Amir. I also gave him Amir's full name and address in Houston.

He said, "I'll pull up his passport when I get back to the office. We'll be able to see where he's been lately. That should help some."

Tom ordered dinner for both of us. It consisted of lamb stuffed with zucchini and a salad dish called fattoush. I quickly realized how hungry I was. It was a great dinner – so far, the best thing about Beirut. I thanked him and said that I would let him know if I learned anything more.

He got up to leave and said, "Okay, John, you sit tight, and I will call you in the morning. I'm going to talk to some people. Does your cell phone work here?"

"No idea, I haven't tried it."

Tom said, "Here is my number, try it."

Tom's phone rang after a twenty-second delay.

"Okay John, looks like we are connected. I'll be in touch."

Chapter 12

I called Karen. She answered on the first ring, "Hello."

"Karen, it's John. Is everything okay?"

She responded, "Yes, we're fine. I haven't heard anything from Amir, neither has his office."

I said, "Karen, I found Amir. He met with some men here. He also is with the dark-haired woman that he picked up at the shopping center in Houston. I tried to follow them here in Beirut but ran into some problems and lost them."

"What kind of problems?"

I said, "My driver and I were shot at. However, I don't attribute that to Amir or his associates here. We just happened to be in the wrong place at the wrong time."

She said, "Oh, John. That's terrible. I don't want you to be hurt. I think you should just come back."

"No, I'm here and I am going to find out what's going on. I think Amir is in danger. I agree with your initial view that he is mixed up with some bad characters. The Embassy here is going to try to help."

She responded, "John, please be careful."

"I'll be fine."

She said, "What about this woman? Be honest with me, John. Is Amir having an affair?

I said, "I honestly don't know, Karen, but I intend to find out. When I saw them, it looked like it was all business."

I hung up and fell into bed. In seconds I was in a deep sleep.

At six o'clock in the morning, my cell rang.

"John, is that you?"

"Yes, who's this?

"It's Williamson. Your buddy flew to Paris last night and is on his way to Mexico City as we speak. I briefed the FBI rep here at the Embassy. They will be tracking him and should know when he re-enters the U.S. What's your plan, partner?"

"To be honest, I don't have one. I could go to Mexico City, but what then?" I said, "I have no idea what his next step might be."

"I hear you. Don't take any more trips around town. Keep me posted on what you decide."

"Roger that." I hung up.

I pondered my alternatives. If I stayed, what could I accomplish? On the other hand, I could go back to Houston and wait. I felt a bit relieved that the FBI was aware of the possibility of an illegal shipment. But there were still too many unanswered questions. Why did Amir come to Beirut in the first place? Surely, he couldn't expect to smuggle something dangerous on commercial flights. Why did Amir leave his car in Brownsville? If I followed Amir to Mexico City, how would I even find him? To quote Donald Rumsfeld, "I didn't even know what I didn't know."

I called Karen again and briefed her on what happened. She had still heard nothing from Amir. I told her to call me immediately if she did. I also reminded her to tell no one, even Amir, where she was. She agreed.

I went downstairs and had breakfast. I was hoping to see one of the people that had been with Amir the day before, but no such luck. I decided to go back to Texas and pick up Amir's trail in Brownsville. It wasn't a great plan, but better than doing nothing.

I went to the Concierge's desk and asked the very attractive Lebanese girl working there to make reservations for me to fly to Houston, preferably on Qatar Airlines. Flying on that airline was the most enjoyable part of this wild goose chase so far. She booked me on a flight leaving in the evening to Doha and on to Houston.

I called Tom Williamson and briefed him on my plan. He agreed to let me know if anything developed at his end. I thanked him for his help.

Ahmed asked if we could make a brief stop at his home on the way to the airport. He said he wanted me to meet his family. I said, "Of course, we have plenty of time."

Ahmed lived in a modest apartment near the hotel. He introduced me to his wife, Alaa, and his son, Abdullah. I could tell he was very proud of his family. They all spoke excellent English, especially Abdullah. He attended the American University of Beirut, which he explained was rated as not only the best in Lebanon, but also one of the best in the world. Abdullah said, "I plan to be a medical doctor. The medical school at AUB has dealings with some of the best medical schools in America."

I asked, "Is the instruction in English or Arabic?"

He said, "The official language for instruction is English, but most of the students are from the Middle East, so we speak Arabic a lot."

They insisted that I have something to eat with them. It was a simple meal with kabobs, rice, pita bread and baklava for dessert. They treated me like a king. I thanked them profusely as we left.

Ahmed took me to the airport. He had already replaced the rear window. He showed me a slug he had dug out of the center console. Six inches to the left or right and one of us would have been hit.

When we arrived at the airport, Ahmed gave me his card. "Mister John, here is my number. Have a safe trip home. Call me if you come back to Beirut and I will show you the good things about my country."

He gave me a hug and watched me enter the terminal. I changed my mind, the Qatar Airlines flight wasn't the best part of this trip, meeting Ahmed was.

Chapter 13

The flight home was uneventful. I was now an expert on how to get around in the Doha airport. It had opened in 2014, replacing the older international airport nearby. This time I had more opportunity to wander around waiting for my flight to Houston. I was even more impressed than before by the facilities at the airport. Qatar had obviously made good use of its revenues from oil and gas.

The flight to Houston was on time. I had become a global services member, which allowed me to bypass the lines for immigration and customs. The officer looked through my passport and obviously noticed the stamps I had received over the past several days. He asked me, "What were you doing in Lebanon, sir?"

"I was there on business."

"What kind of business?"

"I'm a private investigator. I was looking for a missing person."

"Did you find who you were looking for?"

"Well, yes and no. I found him, but then I lost him again."

"Why did you leave if you lost him again?"

"He went to Mexico."

"Did you bring anything back with you? Have any booze, jewelry, guns?"

"No."

He looked at me like he wanted to say, *"Remind me not to hire you to find somebody for me,"* but instead he said, "Welcome home."

I found my truck and left the airport. As I drove to the cashier window as I exited the parking lot the parking attendant noticed my Purple Heart license plate and told me there would be no charge. She smiled and said, "Thank you for your service." What a great country!

I called Karen. She still had not heard from Amir. I made quick calls to my sister and my mom. Everyone was fine. I drove home.

Pal and Mary were both very glad to see me. Pal acted as though I had been away for years. I'm told dogs have no sense of time. He jumped up on me and licked my face. Then he circled around and around. Mary, on the other hand, showed that she missed me with a big hug and kiss as well as a great dinner that included a sirloin steak, baked potato, spinach and some warm corn bread that she had just made. She topped it off with some fresh strawberries.

Sitting at Mary's table was pure joy. It made me appreciate my life in Texas and the U.S.A. I told Mary about my trip, less the part about almost being killed. I told her I was going to Brownsville tomorrow to try to pick up the trail of the person I was tracking. She welcomed the opportunity to keep Pal longer.

After dinner, I went to my apartment, took a hot shower, and collapsed into bed with Pal on his rug next to the bed. Ten hours later, I awakened to my cell phone ringing.

"Hello, Remington here."

"Hey Ranger, it's Tom from Beirut. How was your trip home?"

"Hi Tom, it was fine. I am headed to Brownsville today to try and reestablish contact with my target."

"Don't be surprised if you hear from the FBI. They, along with our other friends here, are taking a real interest in your situation."

His veiled reference to his "other friends" suggested that the CIA was also involved.

I said, "Thanks for the warning order. Call me if you have any other info you can share."

Williamson said, "Roger that."

Chapter 14

I left early to beat the morning rush in Houston. I felt better having my weapon with me thanks to Texas's concealed handgun law. I went south on US highway 59 and six hours later in was in Brownsville, Texas. It is one of the poorest areas, not just in Texas, but also in the entire country. The people, on the other hand, are very friendly. I noticed it immediately when I stopped to fuel up the truck. I asked the attendant for directions to the airport. He came outside and pointed the road to take and shook my hand. He even offered to lead me there, but I declined his kind offer.

I drove into the parking lot at the airport. It took less than five minutes to realize that Amir's Mercedes was not there. What now? I sensed another dead end.

I went over in my mind what I knew to be fact. Amir left home in his car a week ago. He flew to Houston from Brownsville the same day and caught a flight to Beirut. What the hell did he do with his car? What could have happened to it? I needed some kind of a theory to prove or disprove. I drew a blank. Maybe the car was stolen from the airport, possible but unlikely. Maybe he parked it somewhere away from the airport to keep it safe and out of the weather. After all, it is a very expensive car.

I spent the next several hours looking in the covered parking garages all over Brownsville – nothing. I needed help. I called Captain Fortis.

"Hi Cap, guess who?"

"Gee Remington, I would have taken a vacation if I had known that I wouldn't get something to do for you for a whole week."

"Very funny. Well, since you offered, I could use some help."

"I'm waiting with bated breath," he said.

I told him the whole story, including the shooting part in hopes he'd feel sorry for me. He listened, and then said, "May you live in interesting times. What do you want from me?"

"Would you give the police chief here in Brownsville a call and tell him that I'm a good guy that deserves some help."

"You want me to lie?"

"Well in a word, yes."

"Okay," then he hung up.

I waited an hour to give Fortis time to make the call before I showed up at the main Brownsville police station on Jackson Street. When I told the desk sergeant who I was and asked to see the Chief, I was politely told to have a seat. A few minutes later, a handsome well-dressed Latino-looking man came out and said, "John Remington, it's a pleasure to meet you. I'm Tony Rodriquez, Chief of Police in our great little city."

"The pleasure is mine, Chief. Thanks for seeing me."

"Come on back and let's talk in my office."

When we got to his office, he asked if I would like some coffee. I told him I would.

"Cream and sugar?"

"The works, please."

He used his intercom to ask his secretary to bring us two coffees with lots of cream and sugar.

The Chief turned to me and said, "I got a call from Captain Fortis in Houston, who told me you were a pain in the ass, but as a wounded war vet, I should feel sorry for you and help you out." He laughed and said, "Just kidding, how can I help?"

Our coffees came, delivered by a very attractive woman. I smiled. She smiled and left. The Chief didn't seem to be in a hurry, so I gave him the full version, including the shooting part. He listened intently.

"No laws broken here, at least not yet. Let's see what we can find out about that car. Give me the type and license number."

I did. He wrote it down and then called someone at the airport. I assumed it was one of his officers. He gave him the information and asked him to check the cameras and see if that car entered or left the airport from last Wednesday until today. While we were waiting, we theorized what might have happened if the car was never at the airport. I told him that I had checked the parking garages without success. Thirty minutes later his phone rang. He listened, and then said, "You're sure, thanks."

"No luck, the car was never at the airport, not at the terminal or the parking lot."

"Well, Chief, any ideas?"

The Chief stroked his chin and said, "A couple. You said he caught a flight on Wednesday morning at eight o'clock. He must have gotten to the airport somehow. How about by taxi?"

The Chief called someone he called "Chico" at the yellow cab company and asked if there had been a man dropped off early last Wednesday, probably at the United Airlines door. He looked at me and repeated what he was being told by Chico, "No single man, just a couple."

"That could be it. Where did they come from?"

The Chief repeated the questions to Chico. I could hear the answer from where I was sitting, "The border."

Chapter 15

I thanked the Chief for all his help and gave him my card. He said he would call me if anything new turned up related to Amir or his car.

It was now apparent that Amir and maybe the dark-haired woman had driven into Mexico, left the car there, crossed back into the US on foot, taken a cab to the airport, and flown to Houston and then on to Beirut. This was very likely tied to the "dangerous shipment" that Karen had heard the two men and Amir talking about the day before she called me.

I had just pulled into the Vermillion restaurant off Highway 77 for some Mexican food when my cell phone rang.

"Remington," I said.

"This is Special Agent Roberts from the FBI. I would like to meet with you. Where are you?"

"I am in Brownsville. That sounds like a very good idea."

"I figured that is where you might be. I'll be there in an hour. Where can we meet?"

"I just sat down to dinner at the Vermillion Restaurant on Highway 77. I'll wait for you here."

Getting the Feds involved at this point was fortuitous. My alternative was to sit at the border crossing in Brownsville waiting for Amir to come back or simply wait for something else to happen. In the meantime, I enjoyed a great enchilada dinner with a side of guacamole. I passed on the margarita until after my meeting with Roberts. My story was sufficiently bizarre without him thinking I was also under the influence.

Roberts rang my cell. "Mister Remington, I am walking into the restaurant now."

"I'm waving at you from the table to your right," I said.

Roberts was not an imposing figure. He was barely five foot seven, skinny as a rail and looked to tip the scales at about 140 pounds soaking wet. He reminded me of Woody Allen. His hand was small and sweaty as we shook. Well, he wasn't my image of an FBI agent, but maybe he was really smart. It was his meeting, so I waited for him to start.

"How's the food here?"

"Fantastic."

At that moment, a waiter appeared and asked him what he would like. He ordered a salad and hot tea. Who orders a salad and hot tea at a Mexican restaurant?

"Mister Remington, you are a busy guy. I read about your escapades in Beirut and would like to hear the whole story directly from you."

I spent the next thirty-five minutes going over the entire course of events from the first meeting with Karen in my office to the meeting with the Chief here in Brownsville, including the shooting in Beirut.

"That's quite a story. What are you going to do now?"

"Frankly, I have no idea. I was pondering that exact question when you called me," I said.

"As you can appreciate, when someone starts talking about dangerous shipments, especially involving the Middle East, we get very interested. Based on the report from Beirut, we have put Mr. Lahoud on a watch list. We know he entered Mexico two days ago. Of course, this may just be some kind of a crazy business deal, but we're not taking any chances."

"I had the same thought, but the botched kidnapping and the shootout in Dallas make me think otherwise. I'm sure there is a connection there."

He said, "Who knows, but in any case, we are taking this very seriously and will find Mister Lahoud."

"How can I help? My client wants me to find her husband. She is convinced that he is into something bad, and the family is in danger."

"We're keeping everything dealing with this one very close hold, so don't expect me to keep you in the loop. If you get more information, call me immediately. Frankly, I think you should go home and let the professionals handle this."

I bristled at that remark, but let it pass. I told myself that we were on the same team.

He gave me his card, finished his salad and left.

As I watched him leave, I had mixed feelings. On the one hand, I was glad the FBI was involved. They had the capability to track Amir and watch the border. On the other hand, I felt like I had too much invested in this case to follow Special Agent Roberts advice and stand down. In fact, the more I thought about it, the more I resented being summarily dismissed. I compared the attitude of Chief Rodriquez to that of Special Agent Roberts and decided there was no comparison. Roberts was a horse's ass.

Chapter 16

As I drove back to Houston, I decided I should talk to my client. I called Karen. She picked up immediately.

"Hi Karen, it's John Remington. How are you?"

"Oh John, I am so glad you called. I have heard absolutely nothing and am worried sick about Amir. I just know something bad has happened to him," she said.

I said, "I'm driving back to Houston from Brownsville and thought I should update you on everything. First, it appears Amir is okay. According to the FBI, he flew to Mexico from Beirut two days ago."

"The FBI is involved? Does that mean Amir will be arrested?"

"Karen, I can't tell you what will happen. It all depends on what Amir has done or does in the days ahead. There is no evidence that he has broken any laws yet, but frankly, the fact that he has not called you back is not a good sign."

I briefed her on my conversations with Chief Rodriguez and Special Agent Roberts. I told her about the car and the taxi, including the presence of the dark-haired woman.

"It sounds like Amir is romantically involved with this woman, John."

"It's certainly a possibility, but I honestly don't know. I have seen them together twice. Neither time did either of them show any affection or other indication that they were involved romantically."

"John, should I just go home? Do you really think Thomas and I are in still in danger?"

"I would feel better if you stayed there until we know more."

"Okay, but would you check on the house when you get back to Houston? There is a key hidden under a flowerpot on the back porch."

I agreed and drove straight to the house when I got back in town. It was dark when I arrived. I found the key and checked the house. Everything seemed to be as we had left it last week. As I drove off, I noticed a set of headlights come on around the corner from the house. By the time I reached I-610, I was sure the vehicle was following me. I set the H&K on the seat next to me and continued to observe the vehicle. I stopped at a red light. The vehicle stayed several cars behind me. It was a black SUV with two men in the front seat.

I didn't want them to know where I lived, so I didn't go home. I needed to find out who they were and why they were following me. I pulled into the parking lot of a bar called Zippy's and went inside trying to act as if I had no idea I was being followed. When I was inside, I looked out the window. The Black SUV pulled into the back of the lot and cut off its lights. The two men remained in the vehicle.

I went through the kitchen and out the back door, and then circled around the parking lot. I thought about who these guys might be. Maybe they were the guys that tried to kidnap Thomas or maybe they were the FBI following up on the information I had provided to Roberts. I chambered a round in the H&K just in case, put the safety on, and slipped the weapon into my holster under my shirt on my right hip.

I approached the SUV from a rear oblique angle hoping to stay in the blind spot if the driver was using his mirrors. The parking lot was dark. I could see the windows were down on the SUV and I could hear the two men talking in Spanish. I concluded that they probably weren't FBI. I memorized the Texas license number, CM4450.

I leaned in the window and said in Spanish, "Good evening, gentlemen, why are you following me?"

They were taken totally by surprise but reacted quickly. The man on the passenger side was about thirty-five years old, very fat with a mustache and long black hair. He raised a sawed-off shotgun that he was holding in his lap and tried to reorient it toward me. I grabbed the barrel and yanked it out the window just as he fired. The blast was deafening, but the pellets went over my right shoulder. My right ear was ringing. I smashed the butt of the shotgun into his face directly across his nose. Blood gushed. He grunted in pain, but still tried to grab the weapon. I had full control of it and slammed the butt into the side of his head.

The driver had a handgun, but his partner was blocking his having a clear shot at me. Suddenly, the SUV lurched forward and made a hard left turn. The driver fired six rounds in rapid succession from a large caliber handgun. I hit the ground when the first shot rang out. I heard all of the rounds snap over my head. I brought up the shotgun to a firing position, but before I could fire the SUV went between two parked cars and onto Taylor Street careening off a parked car in the process. Seconds later it was racing down the street and out of sight.

Several people came running over. When they saw the shotgun, they back off. I told them to stay away until the police arrived. Within a few minutes, I could hear a police siren. I called

Captain Fortis and reported what had happened. He told me to wait there, and he would come.

The first HPD officers to arrive were cautious to say the least. I stood where the whole incident had occurred with the shotgun and my H&K on the ground. They exited the car with their weapons drawn. They told me to move away from the weapons and lie on the ground with my hands behind my head, which I did. I told them that the handgun was mine and that there were two extra magazines in a pouch on my left hip. I told them that I was a licensed PI with a concealed handgun license. They handcuffed me and searched me. I told them that I had notified Captain Fortis, and he was on his way. By this time two additional patrol cars had arrived, and the parking lot was ablaze in flashing lights.

I sat in the back of one of the patrol cars while the officers cordoned the area and began taking statements from bystanders. Finally, Fortis arrived and told the officers that had handcuffed me to take them off. As I got out of the car, his first words were, "Another fine mess you've made here, Ranger. This is Houston, not Fallujah."

I said, "For a few minutes there, it could have been."

"You are a magnet for trouble, Ranger."

I responded, "On that we can agree."

He said, "Were these the same guys you think tried to kidnap the kid at the school?"

"I'm almost certain it was. It was definitely the same SUV, but it had a different license plate. This plate was Texas CM4450. This time I got a real good look at both of them. The passenger and I had a tug of war for that shotgun. His finger prints are all over the stock."

Fortis said, "That's helpful. It was sure nice of you to hang onto it, thank you very much."

I said, "You're welcome."

He got on his handheld radio and relayed the information I had given to him. He pointed to a guy in plain clothes, who had joined us during Fortis' call and said,

"Talk to Myers, he'll take it from here."

Myers said, "Billy Myers, howdy."

I said, "John Remington."

Myers looked like a classic Texas good old boy. He was about six four, 250 pounds. He was wearing starched jeans, a white shirt and sport coat covering his shoulder holster. His black Justin cowboy boots were shined. When he opened his mouth, it was immediately obvious that he was no dummy.

We sat in his unmarked car and went over every detail. An hour later, he told me to follow him down to HPD headquarters and look at some mug shots. When we arrived, he asked me to write out a statement on the incident. When I finished the statement, Myers brought me over to the computer. I spent the next two hours looking at the mug shots.

I found the passenger who I took the shotgun away from pretty quickly. His name was Manuel Romero. He was a Mexican national who had served time for assault and had been deported. I spent the next ninety minutes looking for the driver, who was the one who fired the shots. I couldn't find him.

Chapter 17

I drove home rethinking how I should have handled the two thugs that were following me. I felt like I had made a big mistake by approaching the SUV. Fortunately, no one was killed, especially me, but I missed the opportunity to find out who they were working for and why they were following me.

I went straight to my apartment, undressed and fell into bed. The adrenalin rush had subsided and now I felt exhausted. I went to sleep immediately.

Birds singing and bright sunshine streaming through the window I had forgotten to close before going to bed awakened me. I needed to clear my head. What better way than to take a good run? I put on my Brooks running shoes, shorts and a tee shirt and I went upstairs to pick up Pal. He was anxious to go and brought his leash and rubbed it against my leg. I clipped it on, and we set off.

Since being shot in Afghanistan, I had been able to build back up to a healthy five-mile run. I went easy for the first mile with an eight-and-a-half-minute pace. I steadily picked up the pace so that I ran the last mile in about six minutes. I felt okay about it despite the fact that I was still slower than I had been when I was in the Ranger unit. I recalled that to even qualify for Ranger training, one of the requirements was to finish the five-mile run in less than forty minutes. I had worked up a good sweat and felt better than I had in a week. One of the good things about running is that it requires no real preparation or special gear, except a good pair of shoes.

After I showered and changed into my work uniform; jeans, black boots, and a tee shirt under a short-sleeved dress shirt worn with the shirttail out to cover the H&K Compact on my right hip and a carrier with two magazines on my left hip. I checked myself out in the mirror as I walked out. I looked good.

I went upstairs to see Mary, who insisted I have breakfast. Three eggs over easy, some crisp bacon, toast and jam, two cups of coffee with lots of milk and sugar – nirvana! After eating, Pal and I went down to the office. I sorted through the mail. Besides a bunch of advertisements, there was a nice check from a law firm that I had done some work for two months ago. I was beginning to wonder if they were ever going to pay. I guess that slow pay is an acceptable business strategy for law firms.

There were no emails of significance. My sister sent a picture of her family with Dad and Mom on the beach in Galveston.

A few hours later, I received a call from Fortis asking me to come by and meet with Detective Myers at HPD headquarters on Travis Street. I left Pal with Mary and drove the truck to link up with Myers. The morning rush hour was over, but Houston traffic was never very light except late at night or on Sunday. I parked a block away and walked to the headquarters. I identified myself and asked the receptionist for Detective Myers. She told me to have a seat.

In about five minutes, Myers appeared and said, "Morning Remington, how's it going?"

"I'm fine, better than last night."

He replied, “Me too, come on back. We’re going to see the captain.”

Myers picked up a folder on the way to Fortis’ office.

Fortis was dressed impeccably. He had on a lightweight gray suit, white shirt and maroon tie. He was all business. No joking this morning. He said to Detective Myers, “What have you got, Billy? You can share it all with Rambo here.”

“Well, sir, we confirmed Remington’s ID of the guy who was wielding the 12 gauge. His name is Manuel Romero. As I told Remington here last night, he’s illegal, was picked up on an assault charge six months ago, served 30 days and ICE deported him. No known address, we didn’t know he was back in the States. We’ve had an APB out on him, and the SUV since Remington picked him out of the book last night.

He showed me the mug shot again and asked if I was certain that this was the man. I said, “That is definitely the guy, but he looks a lot different today with a broken nose and a large lump on the right side of his head.”

Myers snickered and said, “The license plate belonged to a yellow Mazda coup, not a black Suburban. You had the number right. There was another witness that saw the SUV sideswipe a car leaving the parking lot and confirmed the number. The Mazda owner didn’t know the front plate had been stolen until we called her this morning.”

I asked if they had recovered any slugs or shell casings. Myers confirmed that they had only found five .45 caliber shell casings from the parking lot. I had either miscounted, or one had stayed in the vehicle or was lost. They had only recovered two slugs; both had hit a parked car and flattened out. The .45 looked like a dead end. The shotgun is a Winchester 1200 with a pistol grip, made in 1975. It was reported stolen from a home in El Paso in 1990. The barrel was cut down to 16 inches. It had five triple ought buck shells in it with one in the chamber.

Fortis said, "That would have taken your head off if he had gotten it aimed at you." I nodded.

"My right ear is still ringing. That's a nice gun, can I have it?"

Fortis rolled his eyes and spoke up, "It's evidence and even if it wasn't, it's illegal because they cut off the barrel."

I said, "You sure have become a stickler since they promoted you to Captain. You used to be a cool guy, now you're no fun at all."

Fortis said, "Now John, please go home and don't cause me any more grief. I'm beginning to get the shakes when your number comes up on my phone."

Myers snickered again. I left.

Chapter 18

The traffic was heavy when I left the police headquarters downtown. The only good thing about it was that it provided an opportunity to think while I sat in traffic. Despite all the craziness, I still had not found nor protected Amir. I decided that he was probably somewhere in Mexico. I knew the FBI was looking for him and felt some level of confidence that he would be nabbed when he re-entered the country.

The other sort of good thing about heavy traffic is that you can make phone calls. My truck served as my forward command post. I called Karen and told her what had occurred the night before and about my meeting with the police this morning. She said, "Oh, John. That is terrible. Are these the same men that were at the school?"

"Seems likely, but I can't be sure. The driver may also have been in the SUV at Joan's house. I'm glad they didn't get hold of Thomas. These are bad guys."

She asked, "What should we do now? "

"You should definitely stay put. I will stop by and check on the house. I will also stay in touch with the authorities and let you know as things develop. Enjoy Hot Springs. Go visit the gangster museum."

I had been shot at three times in the last week. I was beginning to feel like my switch from the Army to being a private eye was not as different as I had thought it would be, except that I seemed to be on my own now. There was a lot of confidence generated when you knew you had a team of well-trained and equipped soldiers with you in a firefight. Of course, I reminded myself that I had not really been in a real sustained firefight, although the shootout at Joan's house qualified as close combat. I had come out of it without being injured, except for a sore arm. All in all, I felt pretty lucky. I decided to do something different.

I called a good friend, Miguel Monterossa, who was an ex-Navy SEAL whom I had originally met in Afghanistan during a special op we were both involved in. His SEAL team had a snatch mission to capture a HVT (high value target). My Ranger Company was the security force backing them up. It was a night raid with all of us going in by specially equipped CH47 helicopters. It came off almost totally as planned and we celebrated together when we returned to Kandahar. Miguel came from a wealthy Houston family that had the good fortune to own property in the Permian Basin near Pecos that turned out to be awash with oil and associated gas. He was now quite rich and managed the family's investments. Miguel is smooth and intimidating. He stands six three and weighs about 230. He is solid muscle.

"Miguelito, let's go do some shooting. I've gotten myself into some interesting and exciting stuff and want your advice."

"Okay amigo, meet you at the range in an hour," and hung up.

We had a favorite range on Highway 290 that we always used. I brought my H&K and Glock 21, the latter with a combination flashlight and red dot designator. I kept it for the heavy work where being able to conceal it was not a consideration. Miguel was an incredible shot, the best I'd ever seen. I thought I was good, but he was better. He was shooting his Kimber 1911 Gold Match II, the only weapon I had ever seen him carry. We were equally perfect for the first three exercises firing double taps from a holstered position at 10, 15 and 20 yards. At 30 yards, I was 2 inches off the mark, Miguel wasn't. I bought the beer at a small biker bar near the range called, "Roscoe's." I gave Miguel the full story of the Amir case. He listened and asked, "What are you going to do now?"

"No clue. Any ideas?"

"What the fuck, let's go to Mexico and find Amir," he said.

I thought about it for about ten seconds, "Fuckin' A, let's go."

Chapter 19

Miguel picked me up at my apartment in his jet-black Ford Raptor, definitely a cool truck. When we reached Brownsville five hours later, we decided to have dinner at my fnew avorite Mexican restaurant there. I called Chief Rodriquez, and he met us at the restaurant. I introduced Miguel and briefed the Chief on everything that had happened since we were together the previous week.

The Chief said, "I met with Special Agent Roberts from the FBI. He stopped by my office after apparently meeting with you, John."

What did he tell you, Chief?" I asked.

"Roberts didn't share shit with me. He told me that this was Federal business and to stay out of it unless Amir or his Mercedes happened to show up in a traffic stop or caught jaywalking." The Chief referred to him less than affectionately as "el pendejo" (asshole in Spanish).

Miguel and I crossed the Rio Grande River, which is the border, at what is known as the B&M International Bridge. We drove right into Matamoros, the second largest city in the Mexican state of Tamaulipas. It is a tough industrial town with a population of somewhere between five hundred and seven hundred thousand people.

Miguel's family had oil investments in Tamaulipas, so he had good contacts there. He called someone named Carlos, who agreed to meet us at the Bilbao hotel. Miguel said, "Let me tell you something about my friend, Carlos. He is an amazing guy. He is now a detective with the state police, but I first met him when he was a regular cop. We hired him and several other cops to provide security for our people and equipment in the oilfields."

I said, "Can you do that here?"

"Yeah, the cops and the military are the only ones that can legally carry guns, so you end up using them for private security. Mexico is the classic situation where law abiding people can't carry guns, so the only guys out there with guns, except the cops and the army, are the bad guys."

I said, "So tell me about Carlos."

Miguel said, "He is a superstar. He is smart and totally fearless – a great combination. He is especially good for us because he hates the Zetas. His older brother was also a state cop, who was trying to clean up Matamoros and take the city back from the Zetas. One night they went into his brother's house. They made his brother watch while they rape and killed his wife, then they killed everyone except his son who was hiding but witnessed the whole thing. Carlos has vowed to wipe out the Zetas."

When Carlos walked in, he was different than I had expected. He was short, maybe 5'7 in cowboy boots with heels and weighted at least 200. He was built like a fireplug – not really fat, but not all muscle either. He had a thick bushy mustache. What I found unique about Carlos were his eyes. They were dark green and piercing.

Miguel led the discussion. He said nothing about the shipment or the events in Lebanon. He said we were looking for a man, possibly traveling with a dark-haired woman, who came across the border ten days ago. When Miguel described Amir's car, Carlos whistled softly and said, "buen coche" – nice car. I gave Carlos a copy of the picture I had of Amir. Carlos looked at it closely and shook his head. I also mentioned Manuel Romero, as a guy who we thought was involved. Carlos didn't know him either.

Carlos spoke excellent English and seemed anxious to please Miguel. He said he would see what he could find out and get back to us shortly. We checked into the hotel and waited.

At four in the afternoon, Carlos called Miguel and arranged to meet us for dinner at eight at Los Portales restaurant on Calle 6. When we drove up in Miguel's Raptor, a small group of kids gathered around to look at the truck. They all volunteered to watch it while we had dinner.

Carlos was waiting for us when we arrived. He had two bodyguards with him that I assumed were also policemen. We all ordered sirloins rare. My steak was excellent. After some small talk, Carlos said, "You guys are messing with some bad characters. They will kill you and then behead you as a warning to others that try to disrupt their business."

I asked, "Who exactly are we messing with, Carlos?"

He looked around and then said, "I am sure that this involves the leaders of Los Zetas. They are headquartered in Nuevo Laredo here in the state of Tamaulipas. They split from the Gulf Cartel in 2010 and they do not take any shit from anybody. I have to be careful because most of the cops here work for them."

"What makes you think that they are involved with Amir's shipment?" I asked.

Carlos looked around again. "One of my guys saw the car you described being driven here in Matamoros by Manuel Cardenas, a mid-level soldier in Los Zetas. It looked to be headed south toward Tampico."

Miguel finally spoke, "Where do we find Cardenas? Seems like a good guy to talk to about what's going on."

Carlos responded, "Miguel, I think you are out of your fucking mind, amigo."

Miguel asked, "Yes, I am. Does that mean you won't help us?"

Carlos said, "You dumb son of a bitch, of course I'll help you. But you will probably get us all killed."

We left the restaurant at ten o'clock. Carlos's bodyguards were waiting outside. Miguel gave each of the kids that assured him that they had been watching his truck exclusively a few pesos. There was also a van parked next to the Raptor.

Carlos's guys had procured the van. Carlos said that he thought it would be less visible than Miguel's Raptor. Actually, anything would have been less visible than that vehicle. Inside the van, there were two shotguns, two MP5s and two nine-millimeter Berettas and enough ammo to hold off Santa Ana's army.

We checked the weapons. Miguel and ran function checks on the Berettas. Miguel grumbled that he missed his Kimber. Like me, he preferred something larger than a 9mm.

Cardenas lived in small house on a dirt road off Route 2. Carlos knew what he looked like, so the three of us decided to watch the house and wait for him to come home. At midnight, Cardenas showed up driving an old 1995 Chevy. Miguel was driving and pulled up and asked directions to Calle 6 while I crept around the back of the van with the shotgun. Cardenas turned around, looked at Miguel and told him to go fuck himself. About the same time I emerged from behind the van and had the drop on him. Cardenas started to reach for a pistol in his belt, but I hit his arm with the butt of the shotgun, followed quickly by one to the stomach. He gasped for air, doubled over and dropped to his knees. With Carlos's help, we dragged him into the van. Carlos was wearing a balaclava. Only his eyes and mouth were visible. Carlos and I climbed in the back with Cardenas. Miguel drove south on Route 2. Thank God no one seemed to notice. It wasn't a great plan, but it worked.

Chapter 20

Cardenas was starting to breathe normally by the time we pulled into a secluded area off of Route 2. We had agreed that Carlos would not speak or do anything that would give away his identity to Cardenas, since our plan was to keep him alive and release him when he gave us the information we wanted. We searched Cardenas and found two pistols, a Glock 19 model that fired a nine-millimeter round in his belt and a Walther PPK 380 in an ankle holster. He had a K-bar knife strapped to his other calf. The guy was a walking arsenal.

Miguel left the driver's seat and joined us in the back of the van. We used heavy green duct tape to bind his arms and legs. Cardenas looked at me and said in pretty good English, "Gringo, you just signed your death certificate along with these two pendejos. Do you have any idea who I am?"

"Well, Cardenas, yes as a matter of fact we do and if you don't tell us everything we want to know, your Zeta friends will just think the Gulf Cartel got you. Here's the deal, you tell us what we want to know, and this little meeting is between us, and we let you go. If you don't, you're dead."

"Fuck you guys, I am telling you nada."

I was amazed at the speed of Carlos's response. He hit Cardenas so hard in the nose that I thought he broke his cheekbones as well. Blood spurted from Cardenas's nose, and he bent over trying to avoid another blow.

Miguel said, "You're fucking with the wrong guy, Cardenas. I would personally rather kill you because I hate you fucking Zetas."

Now it was my turn to play the good cop. "Okay, Cardenas, let's try this one more time." Cardenas said nothing. He was in obvious pain and was trying to stem the blood flowing from his nose. I gave him a rag and said, "You drove a white Mercedes 600 south out of Matamoros nine days ago. Who told you to do that? Where did you take that car?"

Cardenas said, "You guys have this wrong. I know nothing about a white Mercedes, you've got the wrong guy." Carlos was on him like lightning with another right to the nose followed by a punch to the solar plexus. Cardenas gasped and doubled over.

Miguel pulled out his pistol, pointed it at Cardenas's head and said, "Listen, idiot. We know you drove the car. If you are going to stick with the story that you didn't, I am going to kill you right here and dump your body."

Cardenas seemed to get the message. "Okay, okay, I drove the car, but that is all I know."

Miguel flipped the safety off Beretta. I actually thought Miguel was going to pull the trigger when Cardenas yelled, "No, don't. I know more. I drove the car to a shop near the port at Tampico."

"What shop? Who gave you the order to do that? I asked.

"I don't know the address. I threw it away after I dropped off the car."

Carlos was up again. Cardenas turned his face. Cardenas said, "I know where it is, but I just don't know the address."

I asked, "What about the name of the guy who sent you there?"

"If I tell you that and he finds out, I am already dead."

Miguel said, "You had better trust us, amigo. It is your only chance to live through this little adventure."

"We call him El Lobo or Zeta Cuarenta. He gave me the keys and told me to drive the car to the shop in Tampico and give the keys to a guy called Hummer. That is what I did. Hummer had one of his guys drive me back to Matamoros. Honest, that is all I know."

I asked Cardenas, "Who was with El Lobo when he told you all this?"

"No one. It was just him and me at his office."

I said, "Okay, let's go for a ride. First show me El Lobo's office and then we're going to Tampico. I love the seafood there."

Cardenas directed us to an office building in the center of Matamoros. He pointed to a third-floor window and told us that El Lobo had his office on the second floor right across from the elevator. I said, "You are pointing to the third floor."

Cardenas said, "No, that is the second floor. The first floor is the ground floor."

Carlos nodded in agreement.

We put Cardenas face down in the van, dropped Carlos off near the hotel, and drove south to Tampico.

Chapter 21

It was just getting light when we arrived in Tampico. We propped Cardenas up so he could direct us to the shop where he left the Mercedes. He traveled through some back streets near the port before we finally arrived at the shop. It was a car repair shop on a side street just off of Calle Reforma in the Moralillo neighborhood. No one was there yet, so we waited.

At seven o'clock, two guys showed up in a red Nissan pickup and opened the shop. Cardenas identified the tall one as Hummer, the guy who he had given the Mercedes to and who had told another man to drive him back to Matamoros. Cardenas was very nervous. He told us to not mention his name and be very careful with Hummer, whom he described as a vicious killer. He told us that Hummer got his name because when he was a member of the Mexican Army, he had forced prisoners to lie in front of his Humvee and then had driven over their heads. Cardenas said he had also personally witnessed Hummer decapitate a captured policeman.

Miguel got out of the van and went into the shop. By that time another man, who appeared to work there, arrived. Miguel asked for the jefe (boss). He was sent to the tall guy that Cardenas had called Hummer. Miguel, speaking in Spanish, said that his car needed an alternator and asked if they could replace it with a used one that worked. While he was talking, he looked in the repair bay that had several cars in various states of repair. There was no Mercedes. He could see what might be a separate area in the back that was closed off, possibly for use as a paint shop. Miguel also asked if they could paint his car. Hummer said that he could repair the car, but he couldn't do the painting for another week. Hummer offered to send his mechanic out to pull the alternator. Miguel said he would pull it himself and bring it in for the exchange.

Miguel returned to the van and told us what had happened in the shop. Miguel said, "It is possible the Mercedes is in there, but there was no way to be sure unless we look in that back area."

We decided to get rid of Cardenas, who at this point had outlived his usefulness. We drove out in the country and well off the main road. Cardenas was sure that we were going to deal with him the same way he had no doubt dealt with many others. He was petrified and begged for his life. I told him, "You have one chance to survive. We will let you go, but if we find that you said anything about what has happened, we will hunt you down and kill you." Miguel nodded at him.

"You have my word on my mother's grave, I will say nothing."

Miguel said, "Listen, Cardenas, if anyone asks what happened to you, you say five men robbed you. If you tell El Lobo what really happened, he will know that you spilled your guts and he will kill you for sure, comprende?"

Cardenas said, "Si, si."

I cut the tape and turned him loose.

Miguel said, "We probably should have killed him. He is a liability. He is a killer himself and deserved it."

"You may be right, but I have a problem killing an unarmed person in cold blood, even if he is a bad actor."

Miguel said, "Mi amigo, I love you, but you operate under a code of conduct that is likely to get you killed and me too!"

We drove to the Camino Real Hotel on Avenida Hidalgo. We ate breakfast and planned our next move. It was a great buffet with everything you could want. We decided to have a heart-to-heart talk with Hummer.

After breakfast we drove around Tampico. It is quite a beautiful city. During the early twentieth Century, the city prospered from a major oil boom. It was one of the major oil centers in the world at the time. Abundant money was spent on churches and government buildings. We drove by the cathedral of the Immaculate Conception and the municipal palace. Both were impressive.

We went back to the Camino Real and got a room for the day. We had a typical Mexican breakfast in the hotel's restaurant. We discussed how to proceed. Our plan was to wait for Hummer to leave work and grab him. Miguel was in his element in Mexico. He was totally relaxed and confident. I, on the other hand, was more uptight. We made a good team.

We agreed to meet at four o'clock in the lobby. We went up to our rooms. It had been a long night. Despite the fact that we had not slept for almost twenty-four hours at this point, I couldn't sleep. My mind was racing. What if Cardenas alerted Hummer? Were we in the middle of a terrorist operation that involved Middle East crazies and Zetas? I had lots of questions, but few answers.

I eventually fell asleep. I woke up at three o'clock. Miguel and I linked up at four o'clock sharp. By five o'clock in the afternoon, we were parked near Hummer's shop. His red Nissan pickup was still there.

At six o'clock, Hummer locked up his shop. He and one of his guys got into the pickup and drove off. We followed him. Hummer drove down Reforma Street for about a mile before turning into a small cantina. He and his passenger went inside.

We pulled off the road into a gas station a half a block away where we could watch the pickup and waited.

Chapter 22

Miguel amazed me with his ability to remain quiet and not move a muscle for hours. He would have been an excellent sniper. It was dark when Hummer and his guy finally came out of the bar. They both looked like they had had their share of tequila. We followed them on dirt roads through a poor neighborhood. Hummer finally stopped and let his passenger out, then continued on. We followed him for several miles before he pulled into a dirt driveway next to a small, but well-kept house. We drove by as he went into the house.

We considered our options. We could knock on the door and say, "Hello, we're looking for a white Mercedes that was given to you ten days ago. Could you please tell us where it is and why you have it?" Or we could break into his house and risk being shot, since we knew he was part of the Zeta network and probably armed to the teeth. Or we could wait and try to grab him in the morning when he left for work. We didn't like any of the options, but we decided on the first one.

Since Miguel had already spoken to Hummer, we decided that it would be a mistake for him to show up at the door. That left me, the gringo. Miguel stood to the left of the door out of sight with the Beretta at the ready. I knocked on the door. I heard rustling inside and finally a man's voice in Spanish, "Who is it?" He cracked the door and looked at me. I responded in my best Spanish, "I'm looking for the home of my girlfriend's parents, the name is Sanchez. The directions showed it here."

Obviously, my Spanish was perfect because Hummer responded in broken English, "Fuck you, gringo."

At that moment, Miguel smashed through the door like a freight train. Hummer was caught off guard and as he fell backward onto the floor managed to fire the shotgun he was holding behind the door. Fortunately, the blast went into the ceiling and not into either Miguel or me. I kicked the shotgun out of his hand. Miguel and I both stood over him with pistols pointed at his head.

I said, "Well, it wasn't a great plan, but it worked." Miguel just shook his head.

I grabbed the shotgun, racked it and held Hummer at gunpoint while Miguel checked the house. There was no one else there. The TV was on in the living room. There was a pistol, a cell phone and a set of keys on the table near the door. I put them in my pocket. We searched Hummer but found no more weapons.

"Let's take a ride, Hummer," I said. He was obviously surprised that I knew his Zeta name.

We used the duct tape again to tie Hummer up. Then we tossed him into the back of the van. We drove back to the shop. Hummer said nothing. When we arrived, Miguel used Hummer's keys to open the door and went inside. He opened the bay door, and I pulled the van inside. Miguel had already checked the closed off paint room, but it was empty. Where was the Mercedes?

We dragged Hummer out of the van and sat him in a chair in the small office. I asked him politely, "Mister Hummer, where is the white Mercedes that was delivered to you ten days ago?" He said nothing.

Miguel was on him like a cat on a mouse. It was the Cardenas scenario all over again, except even more violent. Miguel drove the heel of his hand into Hummer's solar plexus. Hummer gasped. Miguel hissed at him, "You had better answer his questions or I promise you will not live through the next hour. We know most of the answers to the questions we're going to ask, so think carefully before you lie to us, Amigo."

Hummer's level of cooperation improved dramatically. Although the blow to the solar plexus made it more difficult to understand him initially, as he recovered he began talking a mile a minute. He told us that he had received orders to install three hidden compartments in the vehicle, which he did. He said the Mercedes had been picked up yesterday.

I asked, "Who gave you the order to install the hidden compartments?"

Hummer hesitated and Miguel started to move. "It was El Lobo. It was him; I swear."

"How did he contact you?"

Hummer responded immediately, "He called me."

What did he tell you the car was going to be used to conceal?"

"He did not tell me that."

Miguel hit him in the solar plexus hard enough to cause him to gasp for air. His eyes rolled back in his head. After about two minutes, Hummer was almost breathing again, when Miguel repeated the question.

Hummer spoke almost inaudibly, "I'm telling the truth. He said that one compartment had to be at least three meters long and one meter wide, the other two had to be one and a half meters long and a meter wide. He said they had to be good enough to pass a border check. That is all he told me."

I said, "Okay, where is the car now? Who picked it up?"

"I don't know where it is, but two guys and a woman picked it yesterday morning. I had never seen them before."

I said, "Let me understand, you turned over a Mercedes 600 worth over one hundred thousand dollars that you had illegally modified to three people you didn't know. You expect us to believe that?"

"El Lobo told me that at nine in the morning a man would come to the office, identify himself Maximo Gomez and tell me that Juan Smith had sent him. I was to give him the keys no questions asked and to call him back when the transfer was made. That is exactly what happened. Honest!"

Hummer showed me the number on his cell phone that he used to contact El Lobo and described the compartments that he had installed in the Mercedes. It sounded like Amir and the dark-haired woman who picked up the car. The other man was Latino and was the only one who Hummer said spoke.

I showed Hummer a picture of Amir. He said it was not the man who took the keys, but looked like the man that was with the woman. "Both this man and the woman stayed outside, so I didn't get a close look at them. I told one of my guys to watch them."

That sounded reasonable to me. I said, "Hummer, this is important. Did the man that was with the woman speak Spanish or any other language?"

Hummer said, "He and the woman stayed some distance away. I never heard either of them speak."

I looked at Miguel. He said, "Okay, Ranger, what now?

I responded, "Samo, samo."

Miguel got very close to Hummer's face and said, "You have one chance to survive this. You say absolutely nothing about what happened tonight. If you say anything, we will know, and I will personally kill you slowly. By the way, if you report this to El Lobo, he will assume that you told us everything. That would be very bad for you as well. If we keep this as our little secret, you might just live long enough to die in bed."

Hummer expressed his eternal gratitude. We dropped him off at his home and headed back north to Matamoros.

Chapter 23

It was our good fortune that we hadn't brought Hummer with us. We encountered three military checkpoints on the way back to Matamoros. When we saw the first one up ahead, we hurriedly hid the weapons under the seats. When the soldiers saw the American passports, they quickly shined their flashlights into the empty van and then waved us through. I had visions of a repeat of what the Marine in Tijuana had gone through when he crossed the border by mistake with guns in his truck.

It was late when we arrived in Matamoros. Miguel called Carlos and briefed him on what happened in Tampico. Carlos said he would have his trusted policemen continue to watch for the Mercedes. We agreed to meet for breakfast at nine at the same hotel. We checked back into the Camino Real.

I reluctantly called Special Agent Roberts. I'm sure he didn't appreciate being called at two in the morning, but I figured that's what G-men signed up to do. When he answered in a sleepy voice, I said, "Special Agent Roberts, this is John Remington. I'm sorry to wake you, but I thought you should have this information immediately."

He responded, “Shoot.”

I said, “Poor choice of words, but here goes.” I told him that we had tracked the Mercedes to a shop in Tampico where it had been configured with hidden compartments. I described the sizes. I repeated it so he could write it all down. I told him that two men and a woman had taken the Mercedes from the shop. The description matched the three I had seen in Beirut, including Amir and the infamous dark-haired woman. I left out our encounters with Cardenas and Hummer as well as the help we received from Carlos.

“Okay, Remington, that’s very interesting. How do I know any of it is true? How did you find out all of this?”

“Good detective work, Roberts. I have good friends in Mexico.”

I could tell Roberts was getting testy, he said, “Look Remington, don’t bullshit me. I could have your ass for withholding information related to a terrorist threat. Now how did you find this out?”

I told him that a member of the Tamaulipas state police, who is a close friend of a friend, had helped get the information. He wasn’t satisfied but didn’t press it further. He said he had to make some calls and would get back to me.

Two hours later, it was Roberts’ turn to wake me up from a dead sleep. I said, “Hello.”

Roberts said, “Bad news, we think your Mercedes crossed the border three hours ago at Laredo. I just spoke to the Border Patrol agent who said there was nothing unusual about the people. They all had U.S. passports and told the agent that they were returning from having dinner in Nuevo Laredo.”

“What the fuck, Roberts. Didn’t you have some kind of special APB on that vehicle. I gave you the plate number and the description.”

"Listen, Remington, I'm getting fed up with you. The car had different plates, so it didn't match the notice we put out. I ran a check and just found out that the plates on the car when it came across were stolen."

"What about Amir, was he in the car?"

"We don't know. Unfortunately the agent just looked at the U.S. passports but doesn't remember the names. We're looking at the video tapes now."

I said, "Roberts, this is a major fuck up. I hope you are checking that border agent out. I'll bet that the bad guys are headed back to Houston."

"We're doing all that. Every cop in Texas is looking for that car as we speak. I'll get back to you if I need anything from you. In the meantime, follow my advice and leave this to us."

"Oh, that's working. I give you the best lead you could possibly have, and your professionals manage to screw it up. I have no idea what is in that car, but I know it can't be good."

Roberts hung up.

I called Miguel in his room and briefed him on the call from Roberts. As is typical of Miguel, he was calm. He said, "It figures, these guys could screw up a wet dream."

Next, I called Karen. I gave her a summary of what had occurred. She said, "John, do you think Amir is helping to smuggle something, maybe weapons, into the country?"

"I don't know, Karen. It is possible he is being blackmailed into cooperating with these guys. One thing I am sure of, Amir is involved with some really bad actors. The Zetas are a brutal bunch."

I told her I would keep her informed and asked her to call me immediately if Amir or anyone else contacted her.

What a missed opportunity! What was hidden in the compartments of that Mercedes? I knew now that this was not some crazy business deal. I also knew that this was not just a drug deal that the Zetas would normally be involved in. They didn't have to go to Lebanon for that. I was less worried about Amir and more worried about an act of terrorism here in America.

Chapter 24

It was already hot and humid when I went downstairs to meet Miguel and Carlos for breakfast. Carlos was waiting in the restaurant drinking a cup of coffee. I ordered a café con leche (coffee with milk) and put three sugars in it. Carlos said, “John, you like coffee with your milk and sugar, no?”

“Si.”

Miguel joined us and we recounted all of the events since we had dropped him off on the way to Tampico.

Carlos grinned and said, “You guys have been real busy. What are you going to do now?”

Miguel and I looked at each other and said in unison, “Good question.”

I said, “Maybe we should head back to Houston. There is a decent chance that these characters will show up there.”

Miguel said, “We need to find that car. Let’s take advantage of what we know. There is one person who probably knows the plan.”

Carlos and I said in unison, “El Lobo.”

Miguel said, “Exactamente!”

Carlos said, “Man, you guys have been lucky so far, but you are messing with some bad fucking shit if you plan to go after El Lobo.

He is the boss here. His Zetas are a very dangerous group. In fact, they are probably the most dangerous group in all of Mexico.

I said, "Are you saying you want no part of it, Carlos? I could see that I had put him on the spot. Carlos was a tough, proud guy.

He responded, "Did I say that? Fuck it, I'm in. I hate those fucking Zetas. We just have to be careful as hell. The Zetas own a lot of the cops, so we can't trust anyone in Mexico to help us."

"Okay," I said, "let's plan this operation. We don't have much time. Let's review what we know. We know where El Lobo works. He was part of the planning for this operation, so he should know what they plan to put in those compartments. He will know where they intended to cross the border and he may know what they plan to do now that they are in the U.S."

Miguel said, "Maybe we need a Judas goat."

Carlos said, "What's that?"

Miguel responded, "Someone who leads you to the target. Kind of like Judas led the Romans to Jesus."

Carlos said, "I get it. You're talking about Cardenas, no?"

I said, "We definitely have some leverage on Cardenas, but he's totally untrustworthy. If he thinks that he can benefit by betraying us, he'll do it. But, I agree that he is our best bet. El Lobo will be ten times harder to grab than either Cardenas or Hummer were."

Carlos said, "I totally agree with you, John. Even after we grab Cardenas, I'm not sure how we use him to get El Lobo. Cardenas is not a major player in the Zetas. He was not a Special Forces soldier in the Mexican army. I think he is someone that they use for simple missions like driving the car to Tampico. El Lobo is not going to respond to Cardenas if he asks for a meeting. In fact, he will be very suspicious of Cardenas even contacting him directly. We better come up with something clever for our friend, the Judas goat.

Miguel responded, "You're right. I've got an idea."

Chapter 25

By noon, we were back in the van sitting down the street from Cardenas's small house. There was no sign of activity. There was good chance that he would not come back until later in the evening. At two in the afternoon, a woman and a small boy walked up to the house. She had a key, opened the door and went inside. This was potentially a major complication.

By five in the afternoon, we were not only tired of sitting in the van, but also hungry as hell. We decided to take a chance and drive to a gas station a few blocks away. Like in the U.S., it had a small shop with snacks and drinks. We loaded up on a bunch of junk food, filled the van with fuel and drove back to our stakeout location by Cardenas's house.

It was about seven in the evening when Cardenas finally showed up. He was alone. He parked his truck on the side of the house and went inside. This was going to be tricky. We could assume that Cardenas was going to be cautious after his experience with us previously. Also, the presence of the woman and child was a potential problem as well.

We considered our options. We could knock on the door and ask him to come outside and speak with us. That might work, but we have to assume he was armed and might not even answer the door. In that case we would have to force our way in and risk a shootout. Alternatively, we could break into the house unannounced and risk not only a shootout but put the woman and child at serious risk as well. Finally, we could wait until he came out and grab him then.

We opted for door number three. The plan was simple. One of us would hide inside Cardenas's truck and wait for him to get in. Since it was my idea, I was elected. I made my way around the neighbor's house. As I came around the corner, I froze. In the darkness I had come face to face with a large Doberman. He bared his teeth and growled at me. My heart was pounding. I tried not to show any fear, probably unsuccessfully. Shooting him was my last resort. I did not want to kill the animal. He was doing what he was supposed to do. I was the intruder. Also, the gunshot would have potentially screwed up the whole plan.

For a brief second, I thought of how a dog whisperer would handle this. Don't look him in the eye. Act submissive. Act dominant. All of the contemplation ended quickly when the dog lunged at me. His entire muscular body was off the ground. I instinctively retreated just before I would have pulled the trigger. In that instant, the dog flipped over backwards. It was on a chain that played out within a few inches of him making contact with me. He picked himself and came at me again barking and growling loudly. The rear porch light came on almost immediately. I backed up and moved swiftly back to the van.

I didn't think the episode with the Doberman was near as funny as Carlos and Miguel did. It was time for plan B. I had them drop me off several houses on the other side of Cardenas's house. My move to Cardenas's truck this time was uneventful.

Fortunately, the truck was unlocked. It would have been unpleasant to have to wait outside the truck. The mosquitoes had attacked me immediately after leaving the van. I climbed into the back seat, killed most of the mosquitoes that had come in with me, and waited.

I was prepared to wait all night if necessary. Fortunately, it was much quicker. Cardenas came out a few minutes later. He climbed into the driver's seat and started the engine. I put the pistol in the back of his head and said, "Buenos noches, guess who?"

Chapter 26

I heard Cardenas groan, "Oh gringo, por favor, not again."

I said, "Yes, but we can make it much easier this time. Maybe, we'll just kill you."

"Please, just keep that crazy one away from me this time."

I said, "Now very carefully, hand me the pistol in your belt. Take it out with your thumb and forefinger very slowly and give it to me. Any mistakes and your brains will be splattered all over the front windshield."

Cardenas complied. I said, "Now, very slowly turn on the dome light and swing your legs over to the passenger seat and pull up you pant legs."

Cardenas did as he was told. As I suspected, he was wearing a small pistol in an angle holster. It was barely visible from above his cowboy boot. I had him remove it just as he had the pistol in his belt. Next came the knife in his other boot. It pays to be careful.

"Okay, Cardenas, now back up and turn to the right."

Cardenas did as he was told.

I said, "See the van? You should recognize it. Pull up next to it."

Miguel opened the van door, then opened the driver's door and told Cardenas to climb down and get in the back of the van. Cardenas did as he was told. He was being extremely cooperative.

When we were all in the van, I got a good look at Cardenas. His broken nose had turned his entire face into a swollen purple, black and blue mess. At that moment, I felt sorry for him. Carlos had his baklava back on. By his body language, it was obvious that Cardenas was petrified of Carlos. Miguel searched Cardenas thoroughly and found nothing more. I was the designated driver. We headed back toward the hotel. It was time to put the El Lobo plan into operation. Miguel said to Cardenas, "Amigo, you're going to like what's coming next."

Chapter 27

We drove the van to a bar near Cardenas's house. There were at least fifty cars in the gravel parking lot. We picked a spot in the back where we wouldn't be bothered or even noticed. We all sat in the back of the van with Cardenas propped against the wall facing the side door.

Miguel said, "Listen, Cardenas, your life only has meaning for us if you help us. Otherwise, we are better off with you dead. There is a famous gringo saying, 'Dead men tell no tales.' Are we communicating here?"

Cardenas nodded.

Miguel continued, "We are going to ask you a series of questions, some that we already know the answers to, some that we do not. If you lie to us or do not fully answer, we will know. If that happens, we are going to turn you over to the masked man here," nodding at Carlos.

Cardenas nodded but was careful not to look at Carlos. It was as if he made eye contact with Carlos, he would be attacked.

Miguel asked, "How long have you worked for El Lobo?"

Cardenas responded, "I've been a Zeta for about two years."

Miguel said, "Is he your direct boss? If not, who do you answer to on a daily basis?"

It was obvious that the question made Cardenas nervous. He was quiet for a few seconds. Carlos moved closer to him, causing Cardenas to jerk away. "I'm waiting, Cardenas. This is an easy question. If you are having problems with this one, you definitely won't do well."

Cardenas said, "El Lobo is the boss here in Matamoros. I think he is responsible for all of Tamaulipas. The guy I work for is called "El Tanque."

"Does El Tanque work directly for El Lobo?

Cardenas said, "Si."

"Was El Tanque involved in the decision for you to drive the Mercedes to Tampico?"

"I don't think so, except that he told me that El Lobo wanted to see me. When I asked him why, he said he didn't know. He said El Lobo wanted me for something he was working on."

I said, "What would happen if you called El Lobo and told him you wanted to meet with him about something important?"

"No, señor, that would be suicide for me and my whole family. He would be very suspicious and either not come or come ready for an ambush."

What Cardenas said made a lot of sense. Something out of the ordinary would alert El Lobo. We had to catch him when he was in his normal routine. Never mind that we had no idea what his routine was.

I said, "I see your point. What is El Lobo's normal routine?"

Cardenas said, "I do not know, señor. He is a big shot. I'm just a small soldier. I have only seen the man a few times."

"When you went to his office to pick up the keys to the Mercedes, tell us what you saw. Were there bodyguards with him? Was the office secure?"

Cardenas started to get very nervous once again. I nodded to Carlos, who grabbed Cardenas by the shirt. Cardenas screamed, "No, no. I'll tell everything I know."

Miguel said, "Cardenas, if you start jerking us around, this will all be over. I told you the questions would get harder. You are in way over your head right now. We would be doing you a favor by killing you rather than making it known you had betrayed the Zetas."

Cardenas realized he was in an impossible position. He said, "The office has a small waiting room with a secretary. When I came in, there were two bodyguards sitting there. I told the secretary that I had been told to report to El Lobo. There was a code box next to the door that she used to enter the next room."

"What was the code she put in?"

Cardenas said, "I do not know that. She was careful to put herself between the box and me."

"What happened then?"

Cardenas replied, "She came back a few minutes later and told me I could enter."

"Did she have to put the code back in?"

"No, señor, she was standing in the door and held it open for me to enter. The next room had another secretary and one bodyguard. I was told to have a seat again. I waited about twenty minutes before El Lobo opened the door to his office and told me to come in."

I asked, "Was there another code box on his office door?"

Cardenas thought for a minute and said, "No, I don't remember seeing one on that door."

I said, "Okay, what happened next?"

"El Lobo said he had a very important mission for me. He told me I was chosen because of my loyalty to the Zetas. He gave me the keys and told me that there was a white Mercedes on the first floor of the parking garage. He told me to drive it directly to the shop in Tampico and give the keys to Hummer. He gave me a small paper with the name and address on it. I told him to consider it done. He said to tell no one about the mission. I left and followed his order."

Miguel said, "What else can you tell us about El Lobo?"

Cardenas said, "That is all I know. He is a big fish and a very dangerous one. He kills at the drop of a hat."

I said, "Do you know where El Lobo lives?"

"No señor, I am certain that he lives in the Fraccionamiento Rio neighborhood, but I do not know the exact house."

Carlos nodded and whispered to me, "It is the nicest neighborhood in town. All the big shots live there."

I asked, "Do you know where El Tanque lives?"

He responded, "Si, but please do not involve him. He is also very dangerous. He will kill me. I have personally watched him cut out eyes and tongues. I even watched him behead a journalist. Besides, he knows nothing of the car."

I said, "Well let's take a drive over to El Tanque's house. Maybe he will invite us in for a nightcap."

Cardenas tried again to convince us to leave El Tanque out of our plan, "Please, señores, this is a very bad idea."

Miguel said, "We specialize in bad ideas, let's go."

Chapter 28

El Tanque lived in an apartment close to the Bilbao hotel. Cardenas told us that he lived on the second floor, apartment 201. There was a uniformed guard of some sort, probably private security, at the front door of the building. There was no parking garage, so the occupants had to park in the lot next to the building.

I asked Cardenas, "Have you been in his apartment?"

He said, "Yes, many times."

Miguel asked, "Do you see his car in the lot?"

We drove through the lot. Cardenas pointed out a new Ford 150 parked close to the building. "That's El Tanque's truck, the red one."

I knew what Miguel was thinking. Rather than creating a scene in the apartment building, we could do essentially what we had just done with Cardenas.

"Can El Tanque see the parking lot from his apartment?"

Cardenas said, "I'm not sure, but I think so."

We decided to wait for El Tanque to come out and then grab him. It was well after midnight. That probably meant spending the night in the parking lot. We secured Cardenas with tape and blindfolded him. He looked like a mummy when Miguel finished with him. He definitely wasn't going anywhere. It also gave Carlos a chance to remove the balaclava that he said was driving him crazy.

We decided that each of us would pull two hours of guard duty while the rest slept. It was just like being back in the Army. We scheduled a "stand to" at first light. That meant everyone was to be awake and ready to go. Carlos volunteered to pull the first shift. At about three o'clock, Miguel woke everyone and told us the guard was checking the parking lot. We all huddled in the rear of the van with all the doors locked. The guard came up to the van and tried the driver's door. He shined his flashlight into the van. The beam did not reach any of us. He moved on.

At a few minutes after five o'clock in the morning, I woke everyone for stand to. People began coming out of the apartment building at about seven o'clock. Carlos was back in his balaclava and Cardenas was positioned where he could tell us when El Tanque came out of the building.

At eight o'clock Cardenas told us that El Tanque was coming. I couldn't believe my eyes. The man was massive. He was at least six four and must have weighed close to four hundred pounds. He was fat, but he also was muscular with very wide shoulders. Now we knew why he had the name "El Tanque" – the tank.

Miguel and I looked at each other. We picked up the shotguns. We threw a tarp over Cardenas and told not to move or make a sound. Carlos climbed into the driver's seat. We were parked about twenty yards directly behind El Tanque's truck.

As El Tanque reached the truck, Carlos pulled the van next to him. Miguel and I were poised in the side door and jumped out with the shotguns pointed at El Tanque. He reached for his pistol. I smashed his hand with the shotgun, and he dropped the pistol, but he wasn't finished. He grabbed the barrel of the shotgun and tried to take it from me. As we struggled, Miguel clubbed him in the head with his shotgun. I was amazed. El Tanque did not go down, instead he flailed at Miguel. Miguel's blow would have disabled, maybe even have killed, a normal person. El Tanque let go of my shotgun, which allowed me to hit him in the head again. That blow staggered him, but he still did not go down. I was beginning to think we might have to shoot El Tanque to get him under control when Miguel delivered a crushing blow with his shotgun. He held it like a bat and hit El Tanque in the back of the head. El Tanque grabbed his head and fell to his knees. By this time, Carlos had come around to assist. We all grabbed El Tanque and literally drove him into the van like a battering ram.

Chapter 29

Miguel grabbed the duct tape and wrapped it around El Tanque's arms and body. El Tanque was still struggling and kicking. Carlos was back in the driver's seat and pulled out of the parking lot. We finally had El Tanque under control thanks to a complete roll of duct tape and two shotguns. El Tanque's head was bleeding. I took a bandage from the first aid kit and pressed it on his head to stop the bleeding.

Carlos and I traded places to avoid Carlos driving around wearing a balaclava. Carlos gave me direction. I pulled the van into an abandoned warehouse that he knew was safe. Miguel and I were exhausted. I felt like we had wrestled a rhinoceros. We propped El Tanque up against the side of the van. He was like a captured animal. I asked him if he spoke English, he shook his head. Miguel told him that life was hanging by a thread. He said that we had gone to great lengths to take him alive, but if he doesn't cooperate with us, we will kill him.

Miguel asked, "Do you know El Lobo?"

El Tanque shook his head.

Miguel grabbed El Tanque's finger and twisted it. El Tanque screamed and squirmed. Miguel asked him again if he knew El Lobo. This time El Tanque nodded vigorously.

Miguel said, "Now that wasn't so hard, was it? Let's try another question. Do you know where El Lobo lives?"

El Tanque asked, "Who are you guys?"

Miguel said, "You don't get to ask questions. Answer the fucking question I asked you."

El Tanque said, "Yes, I know where he lives. If I tell you and El Lobo finds out, he will not only kill me, but he will have my parents, my sisters and my wife killed as well."

I told him in my best Spanish, "Look El Tanque, if you cooperate with us, no one will ever know, and you will go free. If you don't, we will make sure that El Lobo knows that you betrayed him, or we might just kill you. You see, you really have no alternative. Now we are going to take a ride over to Fraccionamiente Rio and you are going to point out El Lobo's house."

The Fraccionamiente Rio neighborhood is located on the Mexican side of the Rio Grande. It had been the scene of a major gun battle recently between the cartel and the Army. It is directly across the river from the University of Texas campus in Brownsville.

El Tanque directed us to El Lobo's house. He said that we would need an army to attack the house. When I saw the house, I was inclined to agree with him. There was an eight-foot wall with guard posts at each corner and a guard shack at the gate. Miguel and I quickly concluded that trying to take El Lobo at his house was too risky.

We went back to the abandoned warehouse to regroup and decide what to do now. It appeared that our only options were to take El Lobo at the office or say screw it. In either case, we had no more use for either Cardenas or El Tanque.

Carlos watched El Tanque as well as Cardenas, who were still under the tarp, while Miguel and I stepped out of the van. We had just concluded that we didn't have the horsepower to take El Lobo. We called Carlos out and asked him if we could count on the police to help take El Lobo. He said, "You got me and one other that I totally trust, that's it. In a word, the answer is no."

We decided to release Cardenas and El Tanque and then return to the States. We headed back to El Tanque's apartment with the intent to leave him in his truck tied up so that we had enough time to drop Cardenas off and get back across the border. All that changed when El Tanque's cell phone buzzed from inside the van.

Chapter 30

Miguel picked up El Tanque's cell phone. He looked at it, the caller ID said, "El Lobo." Rather than try to have El Tanque answer the call, Miguel answered the call, "Si."

A woman said, "Lobo will meet you at the Plaza restaurant at noon. Sit in the back near the kitchen."

Miguel responded, "Enterado" (understood).

She hung up.

Miguel told us what the woman, who we assumed was El Lobo's secretary, had said. We concluded that this presented a unique chance to grab El Lobo. Carlos said, "I know that restaurant well. It will be crowded with people having lunch. This will not be easy, but it is better than trying to take him at his house or office."

I said, "We have two hours, let's case the restaurant."

We drove to the Plaza restaurant near the center of town. It was not open yet. In the rear of the restaurant, there was employee parking and a door that Carlos said led to the kitchen. There were trashcans and empty boxes near the back door. There was a lot of activity by employees going in and out of the door.

Miguel said, "I'm going to walk into the kitchen and take a look around. "

We watched Miguel disappear into the building. He was gone for about fifteen minutes. When he came out Miguel was with another man, who I assumed was the owner or the manager. He was wearing a lightweight suit and tie. They spoke briefly at the rear door, shook hands and the other man went back inside. Miguel came back to the van. He said, "That guy was the manager of the restaurant. I told him I was planning a celebration for my mother's birthday. He showed me around. We could pull this off if El Lobo's security is not too elaborate."

The plan was simple. The execution was another matter. Miguel and I would act as guests sitting near where we thought El Lobo would sit. Carlos would take out any security in the kitchen or back door. He would also drive the van after we brought El Lobo out. We decided we had to include El Tanque in the plan, although it increased the risk significantly. If El Tanque was not in the restaurant as ordered, it would alert EL Lobo and he probably wouldn't even come into the restaurant.

We propped El Tanque up in the van and took off his blindfold. Miguel said, "El Tanque, here is your best chance to survive. El Lobo's secretary called you and told you to be at the Plaza restaurant at noon and to sit near the kitchen. If you don't show up, El Lobo and his people will know that you set him up. If you cooperate with us, you can come out of this as a hero."

El Tanque said, "How can I come out of this as a hero?"

I said, "Because we are going to knock you out when you try to come to El Lobo's defense. Actually, we won't hit you that hard, but you need to pretend to be knocked out. You also should know that if you don't go along with us or betray us, you would be the first one shot. That is a promise. I will have a gun pointed at you the entire time."

Miguel said, "Are you in or out?"

El Tanque thought for a moment then said, "I'm in."

Chapter 31

We drove back to El Tanque's apartment to get his truck. I drove it back to the restaurant. The more I thought about what we were about to do, the more concerned I became that it might turn out to be a complete disaster. El Tanque was a huge risk. His size was a big part of what bothered me. I remembered how hard he was to bring under control when we grabbed him that morning. We would have to shoot him in the head to take him down if he betrayed us. The other major risk was El Lobo's security team. We were counting on them to be average. If they were really good, we could be in trouble. I was also concerned with innocent people in the restaurant being killed if a shootout occurred. Our plan was to pull off the operation without firing a shot.

We watched the restaurant for almost an hour before we entered. No security for El Lobo was apparent. We unwrapped El Tanque. Miguel and I followed him into the restaurant. He sat at the table nearest to the kitchen. So far, he was acting as planned. Miguel and I sat close, but not right next to his table. We hoped that El Lobo's bodyguards would take the closest table.

At two minutes to twelve, two husky guys entered and looked around. They were obviously El Lobo's security team. They sat at the table we left open for them. So far, so good. Almost immediately, the person we assumed was El Lobo came followed by another person that was clearly his chief bodyguard. El Lobo was younger than I expected. He was dressed in an expensive white suit with an open collared blue shirt. He was tanned and handsome. He exhibited obvious confidence. He spoke to several other guests as he walked toward the rear of the restaurant. The chief bodyguard sat down with the other two.

We had decided to move quickly before El Tanque might rethink his options and alert El Lobo or his security. As soon as El Lobo sat down, we moved. I kept open cell phone contact with Carlos and told him to go.

Miguel and I had our guns on the three bodyguards just as Carlos entered with his balaclava on and an MP5 in hand. The MP5 sub machinegun is a great weapon for inside buildings. It is relatively small. It fires a nine-millimeter round from a thirty-round magazine. It can be fired in a single shot or fully automatic mode by flipping a selector switch.

Timing was critical. Miguel told the bodyguards to get on the ground with their hands behind their heads. El Tanque jumped up as if trying to help the bodyguards. As planned, Carlos clubbed him with the MP5. It was harder than I thought necessary, but it made for a realistic effort. El Tanque went down and didn't move. So far, so good. Miguel and I disarmed the bodyguards. We had to move quickly, but not miss anything. Each bodyguard had a pistol in either a shoulder or belt holster. All of them had pistols in ankle holsters as well. I hoped we hadn't missed a weapon. The patrons in the room were frozen. You could have heard a pin drop.

Carlos had El Lobo by the suit coat with the MP5 at the back of his head moving him to the kitchen. As planned, Miguel ran ahead to open the van and drive it when we had El Lobo inside. Carlos and I were moving back-to-back with me covering our exit. The kitchen workers were also frozen in place watching as we pushed El Lobo through the kitchen and out the back door. The van was open. We pushed El Lobo in and then climbed in as Miguel raced out of the parking lot. The adrenalin was still pumping like crazy as we turned down the first side street off the main road that ran in front of the restaurant.

After we made three more turns, it looked like we were in the clear. As we approached another main road, we saw three police pickups racing in the direction of the restaurant. Carlos had El Lobo face down in the van. I pulled out our last roll of duct tape and wrapped his arms and legs. Carlos removed a Glock 19 from a holster on his belt. Ten minutes later we were back in the abandoned warehouse.

Chapter 32

Carlos dragged El Lobo out of the van and propped him up against the rear tire. He was very rough in his treatment of El Lobo. He slapped El Lobo hard across the face. It was apparent that he really didn't like El Lobo on a very personal level. I had not seen this kind of anger from him with either Cardenas or El Tanque.

I knew we had to move quickly. Every Zeta and ninety percent of the police would be combing the city to find him. I asked El Lobo if he spoke English. He responded, "Well, of course. I'm a graduate of one of your Ivy League schools, my friend. Let me give you some friendly advice that might save your life. Let me go now before they find you and be assured that they will find you. This is my town. I own it."

I said, "Thanks for the friendly advice. Actually, we will be very happy to let you go as soon as you answer a few easy questions. First question is what do you know about a white Mercedes that was sent to Tampico to let us say, be customized?"

El Lobo responded, "Actually, I prefer Bentleys."

Carlos had no patience for him. He slapped him hard again.

El Lobo shook it off and smiled, "I guess your masked friend doesn't like Bentleys."

I said, "Listen, there is no need for violence here. We are just looking for some information." I knew down deep that El Lobo was a heartless criminal that would have us and our families cut into little pieces given the chance.

He said, "I don't know anything about a white Mercedes."

Carlos had had enough of El Lobo; he rammed the butt of the MP5 down on El Lobo's hand that had been resting on the floor below the duct tape that was wrapped around his body. El Lobo tried to suppress a scream. I could tell that at least two of his fingers were broken as well as the small bones in his hand. Tears were streaming down his face.

I said, "Shall I ask again?"

El Lobo said, "No, you made your point. Yes, I do know about a white Mercedes. It was part of a business transaction. I sent it down to Tampico to be modified so that it could carry certain contraband across the border."

I said, "Good, we're making progress. What kind of contraband?"

He said, "That, sir, I don't know. I was paid to modify the car only and have it ready for pickup."

I said, "I don't believe you." As soon as I spoke, Carlos brought the MP5 up again. El Lobo cried, "No, that's not necessary. Although they didn't tell me, it was obvious that they were planning to transport weapons. They didn't seem like drug smugglers."

I followed up by asking him, "What kind of weapons do you think they were planning to smuggle?"

He responded, "If I were to guess, I would say a combination of weapons. There were smaller compartments for small arms, but the longer ones would cause one to conclude that in addition to RPGs, they might be smuggling shoulder-held anti-aircraft weapons."

Miguel and I looked at each other. If El Lobo was correct, this was a very big deal.

I said, "Who were these guys?"

He responded, "Before your masked man hits me again, let me tell you that I don't know the identity of the client. I hope you can understand that our transactions, which usually involve drugs, are designed to protect both parties. You can kill me, but I can't tell you what I don't know."

I said, "Tell us what you do know."

He said, "I will. Firstly, I've already received payment, so helping you intercept these weapons is actually a benefit to me. I'm not interested in seeing terrorism in the U.S. In some ways it's my second home. Although I can't be sure, I think this deal came out of the Middle East."

I said, "You said you had already been paid by your client. How were you paid?"

"In this case, the funds were transferred to one of our Swiss accounts in Geneva."

I said, "I'm sure that you have been keeping tabs on these guys after they picked up the car. Where did they go? Where and when do they plan to cross the border."

El Lobo hesitated. Carlos picked up the MP5 again. I could tell he wanted to inflict more pain on El Lobo.

El Lobo said, "I don't know where they plan to cross, but I can tell you that it is not going to be in my sector. That means it won't be here in Matamoros or Reynosa. We followed them past Reynosa and handed them off to the next sector to the west. As to when, I have no idea. They may already have crossed."

Miguel, Carlos and I moved out of earshot. I asked them what they thought. Both felt like we had done well to extract this information from El Lobo and that we should get out of

Matamoros as quickly as possible and pass what we knew to the FBI. I agreed. Then I asked, "What do we do with El Lobo?"

Carlos said, "I vote to kill him. He and his men have murdered some of my friends and some good policemen."

Miguel said, "Works for me."

I said, "I've killed people in combat, but I don't kill people that are my prisoners. It may be a mistake, but I'm for turning him over to the authorities if possible."

Carlos said, "If that was a viable option, I would have done it years ago. The guy is untouchable."

I said, "Okay, leave him here and let's get going."

We left El Lobo tied up in the warehouse. Miguel drove us back toward the Camino Real. A block before we got there, we unwrapped Cardenas and kicked him out. I told him it was in his best interests to forget everything he had heard or seen since we picked him up. He enthusiastically agreed.

We pulled into the hotel parking lot next to Miguel's truck. Carlos pulled off the balaclava and said, "I love you guys, but stay out of Matamoros for a while. I need a vacation."

I said, "You have my word on that. Seriously, Carlos, you are a brave guy. I hope we haven't compromised your safety here. If you need help, you know that you can count on us. We are only about six hours away."

Miguel said, "Ditto and get rid of this fucking van right away."

Carlos agreed. We gave the weapons we had back to Carlos along with those that we had captured. After abrazos (hugs), we got into the truck and headed back to the border.

Chapter 33

There was a long line of cars waiting to cross the B&M International Bridge. It took over an hour to get to the front of the line. I used the opportunity to call Roberts with an update based on what we had learned from El Lobo. He didn't answer, so I left a message about the likelihood of weapons including handheld antiaircraft weapons like stingers. I also told him that our contact thought that the Mercedes wouldn't cross the border in either Matamoros or Reynosa. He thought it was more likely that it would be further west, which likely confirmed the information about Laredo being the place where they crossed.

When we pulled up to the crossing point the agent said, "Passports please."

We gave her the passports, which she ran through a machine. Then she asked, "How long have you been in Mexico, where did you go and what was the purpose of your trip?"

We told her we were visiting friends in Tampico and had been in Mexico for three days. She looked back at her machine and then she waved us on.

Roberts called me back two hours later. He said, "We confirmed that your Mercedes crossed the border at Laredo. I just spoke to Border Patrol agent who said there was nothing unusual about the people. They all had U.S. passports and said they were in Nuevo Laredo having dinner."

"Like I told you before, this is a major fuck up. You have a real communication problem between your outfit and the Border Patrol."

"Listen, Remington, I'm really fed up with you and your Mexican friends. Maybe I should be investigating them, and you too."

"Knock yourself out, amigo. When you screw up, find someone else to blame. I give the best lead you could possibly have, and you professionals manage to screw it up. I don't know for sure what is in that car, but I know it can't be good."

No response from Roberts.

I said, "I'll bet that they are headed back to Houston."

"Every cop in Texas is looking for that car as we speak. I'll get back to you if I need anything from you. In the meantime, follow my advice and leave this to us."

Roberts hung up.

I turned to Miguel and briefed him on the call. As is typical of Miguel, he was calm. He said, "Like I told you before, these guys could screw up a wet dream."

We called Chief Rodriquez in Brownsville and briefed him on what we found, including the information from Special Agent Roberts concerning the crossing by the white Mercedes in Laredo. He listened intently, then he said, "I hate to say it, but the Feds could fuck up a wet dream."

Miguel looked at me. I said, "Great minds."

Next, I called Karen. I gave her a summary of what had occurred. She said, "John, Amir is in big trouble, isn't he?"

I told her that there was still much that we didn't know and to call me immediately if Amir or anyone else contacted her.

What a missed opportunity! What was hidden in that Mercedes? I was now convinced that this was terrorism in the making.

Chapter 34

It was late in the day by the time we arrived back in Houston. We talked about various options, including a follow up on the dark-haired woman's apartment. Miguel and I agreed to have breakfast in the morning and decide how to proceed.

Coming home was the best thing that had happened in the past week. Mary Fitzgerald hugged me and insisted that I eat at least six chocolate chip cookies that she had made that afternoon. What could I do? I certainly didn't want to hurt her feelings.

Pal's tail was wagging so fast he could hardly walk. He circled around me and whined like I had been gone for a year. He finally settled down when I sat down at Mary's table to eat the cookies. He was not pleased that I wouldn't give him one. Even after I explained to him that chocolate was very bad for dogs, he still wanted one. I promised him a treat when we got upstairs. Instead, Mary came to the rescue with two treats.

Before I went to bed, I called Captain Fortis and briefed him on everything that occurred. I left out selected violent incidents in Matamoros and Tampico. I told him that Miguel and I were going to watch the apartment complex where Amir and the dark-haired woman had gone two weeks before. It seemed to be the only lead we had at this stage. I gave Fortis the cell number for Special Agent Roberts and suggested he call him and get an update given that it was highly possible that these guys would return to Houston at some point. He agreed.

Chapter 35

Miguel and I met for breakfast at a Starbucks near the apartment complex. I had a blueberry muffin and a cinnamon latte. I had convinced myself that cinnamon was the new miracle food. Not only was it supposed to be good for you, it tasted great too. Miguel had black coffee and an old fashion donut. Properly nourished, we headed off to the apartment complex.

We checked the parking garage to see if the white Mercedes was there. It wasn't. We parked adjacent to the entrance to the parking garage and waited. After an hour, Miguel finally spoke, "This sucks, what is plan B?"

I responded, "I don't know."

Miguel said, "I thought you were the master detective. Now you tell me you have no plan B?"

"That's right."

Miguel said, "Fuck me," and put his head back against the seat.

At two o'clock, we had seen nothing. Miguel walked over to the Starbucks and returned with two lattes and two turkey sandwiches. He didn't appreciate my saying that I really wanted a chicken sandwich. I said, "I was joking."

At four thirty, Miguel said, "Eureka!"

The Mercedes with three occupants drove into the garage. I called Fortis and told him what was happening. Miguel stayed in the truck. I went into the lobby to watch the elevator but heard a continuous horn blowing from outside. I looked out and Miguel was waving at me. I looked and saw the white Mercedes driving down the street. I jumped in the passenger door, and we followed it.

It looked as though there were only two people in the car now. I called Fortis again and reported what was going on. He told me not to hang up. The Mercedes was driving fast and following it without alerting them was almost impossible. I told Miguel to stay with them no matter what. If they saw us, then we'd deal with it.

It didn't take long for them to realize that we were following them. They wanted to get away from us, but not attract the attention of the police or have an accident. We kept them in sight but didn't follow so close that they could make a quick turn and lose us. We both ran a red light and they immediately turned on Hardy Street into a residential area north of city. Miguel was keeping Fortis informed as to where we were.

As we turned another corner, I saw that the Mercedes had stopped. I saw the flashes just before I heard the familiar pop of the AK. One round went through the windshield and shattered the rear-view mirror. Miguel shouted, "Jesus Christ, get down."

As we returned fire with our pistols, the Mercedes sped away again. We had each fired a full magazine. One of our rounds hit the rear window, but it was impossible to know if we had hit one of them. The chase continued north toward the international airport. The Mercedes was traveling over 120 miles an hour at times.

I thought we were going to lose them when an HPD police car passed us and fell in behind the Mercedes. Within a minute, two more police cars joined the chase. The Mercedes continued at very high speed in an effort to evade the police. As they entered a residential area, they sideswiped a panel truck. The Mercedes kept going with the police cars and us in pursuit. One thing about Houston cops is that they have a reputation for never giving up the chase.

A few seconds later, a Harris County Sheriff's car raced past us to join the chase. A police helicopter was overhead as well. I was feeling confident that we finally had them. As we rounded a bend, we saw that a roadblock had been set up ahead of the Mercedes. As we got closer, we saw the Mercedes attempt to go around the roadblock. It careened to the right, hit the curb and flipped. By the time we arrived, there was a firefight ongoing. Rounds were flying everywhere. One policeman was down. Within minutes the firing stopped. Both occupants of the car were sprawled out next to the vehicle.

Chapter 36

Two officers ran over to the officer who was shot. Miguel ran with them and identified himself as a trained medic. They worked feverously to stop the bleeding. In a few minutes I could hear an ambulance approaching from a distance.

The other cops were checking the two occupants of the car. Both had head wounds and were obviously dead.

The wounded officer had two gunshot wounds, one to the lower abdomen just below his vest and another just below the ear. He was conscious when they loaded him in the ambulance, so I was hopeful that he would survive. He had been the first to approach the overturned car when both occupants opened fire.

Captain Fortis showed up about ten minutes after the shooting. After speaking to his other officers and checking by radio on the wounded officer, he came over to us.

I asked, "How's the officer?

"Too early to tell, but so far so good thanks to you," pointing to Miguel who had the officer's blood on his shirt and jeans, "We owe you, thanks."

Miguel nodded.

I described what had occurred at the apartment and the subsequent chase. Fortis said, "Well, for once you two hoodlums did okay. I was afraid you were going to try to take them in the apartment lobby or something. We'd still be picking up bodies."

Roberts arrived about fifteen minutes later in a black SUV with the siren blaring. I gave him an abbreviated version of what had occurred. Fortis led us all over to the Mercedes that was on its top. The two dead guys were still lying beside it. An AK47 was next to one of them. It looked like Amir had been holding a Glock in his right hand. Both had been hit multiple times and were a mess. I looked at the bottom of the car and noticed one of the compartments that had been added in Mexico. It was partly broken open, apparently during the crash. It looked like several Russian Strela handheld missiles were inside. Roberts was on the phone immediately speaking in a hushed voice. He turned to Fortis and told him to secure the area completely and that the FBI was in charge of this investigation. I reminded them that the dark-haired woman was still at large and would not stay in the apartment when all of this hit the news.

By now there were at least ten police cars with flashing lights, three FBI SUVs, yellow tape everywhere, and the coroner's van. A large crowd had gathered. Two news trucks were already on the scene and two helicopters were circling overhead. The quiet neighborhood with its trimmed hedges and beautiful lawns had turned into a zoo.

I called Karen and told her what had happened. I wished I could have been there to console her in person. She was obviously devastated. I told her I would keep her informed of developments, but it was best for her to remain with her sister in Hot Springs for now.

We waited patiently for a pat on the back from Roberts, but it never came. I told myself that success is its own reward.

I asked Fortis to tell me what he could about everything so I could keep my client informed. She would want to know when she could arrange for a funeral and bury Amir. He agreed.

I said, "I'm also very interested in what else is hidden in that vehicle. I've been chasing it and Amir for a couple weeks and it has almost gotten me and some others killed."

Fortis said, "I will tell you if and when they will tell me. Don't count on that happening anytime soon if Roberts stays in charge."

Fortis thanked Miguel again, then pointed his finger at me as if it was a gun and said, "See ya, Ranger."

Roberts insisted that Miguel and I give his people at the scene statements of what had occurred. That was followed by a host of questions by another special agent named Emily Medlock. Fortunately, she started the questions from when we arrived at the apartment complex, so we were able to avoid having to recount all of the events in Mexico that led up to our stakeout this morning. She finally told us we could leave and moved to another vehicle where another FBI agent was interviewing the police officers involved in the shootout.

I dropped Miguel off at his truck. He said, "It's been a pretty slow day, let's try to pick up the pace tomorrow."

I said, "It's a hell of note when we have to rely on the cops to finish things up for us. Actually, I blame most of that on you. If you could shoot straight, we could have nailed them when they opened up on us before the cops even showed up."

Miguel said, "I think I hit one of them and it just probably took a while for him to die. I think I saw one of your rounds hit a tree limb ten feet away from the car. Yeah, I'm sure of it."

I responded, "I was driving and shooting at the same time. All I heard on your side was a bunch of swearing."

Miguel slapped the back of my head and got out of the truck. We agreed to link up the next morning for breakfast.

It was dark when I pulled into my driveway. Mary had held dinner for me, for which I was very grateful. She served me a plate with four lamb chops, mashed potatoes and a large portion of spinach. She added a glass of white zinfandel, which made it perfect. Pal curled up at my feet. I was in heaven.

Mary asked, "How was your day, John?"

"Just another day in the life of John Remington, private eye."

Mary laughed and said, "Are you still hanging around with Miguel. He's such a sweet boy, very handsome too."

I responded, "Yes, we have spent a lot of time together lately. But please don't give him any compliments, he's already a pain."

"Thanks for the great dinner, Mary. You're terrific." She beamed.

I took Pal outside and then we went upstairs to the apartment. I finished reading my emails, which were nothing but trash. I took a long, hot shower and climbed in bed. My mind started racing. I thought about all that had happened in the past few days. I was glad that we not only thwarted the terrorist plot, but also found Amir. That thought made me sad for Karen, but I knew she also felt some sense of closure to know the truth.

Chapter 37

I woke up early. It was going to be a hot sunny day. I could feel the humidity starting to build. *Welcome back to Houston,* I thought. I climbed out of bed, put on my black running shorts, a gray tee shirt, and my Brooks running shoes. Pal was waiting at the door with his leash in his mouth. What a team we are!

The five-mile run took us through Memorial Park and back to the apartment. Pal acted like he could go another five. I fed and watered him before I jumped into the shower. When I finished, I called Miguel and told him I would buy him breakfast at the Starbucks by my place.

He said, "Thanks, that is the best thing I've gotten from you lately. Beats getting shot at."

By nine o'clock, I was ready to meet the day. I walked over to the Starbucks to meet Miguel. I winked at the girl who was taking my order and said, "Two lattes and two pieces of banana bread, please."

She smiled back and asked my name.

"John." She wrote it on one of the cups.

When she called my name, I picked it up. This time she winked at me. I smiled back. I sat down to eat my banana bread. When I looked at the cup, under where she had written "John," she also had written "Barbara" and her phone number. That is when I knew for sure it was going to be a good day.

Miguel walked in a few minutes later. I pointed to the latte and the banana bread. He mumbled, "No, I really wanted a blueberry muffin, and the latte is cold."

Of course, he was kidding, but I seized the opportunity. I went back to the counter and said, "Barbara, I need another Latte and a blueberry muffin, please." I followed up with another wink. She smiled.

I repeated her phone number from memory. I was showing off and she was impressed.

She smiled.

Miguel and I went over the events of the past week. Miguel agreed that allowing El Lobo to live was the right decision. That was important for me to hear because I felt like I had forced my will on both Miguel and Carlos. We had managed to accomplish a great deal without having to kill anyone. We both knew that the Zetas would not have afforded us the same courtesy.

The whole experience had cemented what was already a very strong friendship between Miguel and me. When all the kidding and sarcasm was set aside, we both felt bond of brotherhood that only comes from relying on one another in dangerous situations. It is hard for those who have never had the experience to understand it.

Miguel finished his breakfast and said, "Well, Ranger, I'd like to stay and bullshit with you, but duty calls. I have to devote some time to the family business. We just hired a new drilling outfit that can't seem to get anything right."

I said, “I’ll be in touch with Fortis and maybe Roberts today. I’ll give you a call as soon as I know more. I’m certainly expecting a call from the head of the FBI to thank us for saving their ass.”

Miguel said, “Dream on, brother, but seriously, let me know what they find out about those scumbags.” We walked out together. I got a little wave from Barbara, which I returned.

Chapter 38

I walked back to the office. I just sat down at my desk when the phone rang. It was my mother. "Hi John, this is your mom, remember me?"

"Yes, Mom, I remember you. I was just going to call you," I lied.

"Sure you were. Listen, John, your sister and her husband are coming up for dinner this evening. Your dad and I were hoping you could come too. We haven't seen you for months. We're not getting any younger, you know."

My mother was a master of guilt. I said, "Sure, Mom. That would be great. What time should I show up?"

"This is your home, John. Come anytime. We'll have dinner at six."

"Sounds good. How's Dad?"

"He's fine. He asks about you constantly." More guilt.

"Okay, Mom. Love you guys. See you later."

My parents lived in College Station, Texas. It is about a hundred miles northwest of Houston. It is the home of Texas A&M University, which is now the largest university in Texas having surpassed the University of Texas in student enrollment. It is famous for its football team, its Corps of Cadets, its renowned marching band, and its academics. My dad is a proud Aggie, which explains why he decided to live there when he retired from the Army after thirty-three years of service as a major general. My mom was a teacher, who had taught within the Department of Defense system when we were overseas and in various school districts in the States.

Like my father and my sister, I graduated from A&M. I have fond memories of my time as a cadet there and always enjoy going back, especially during football season. The Aggies are now part of the SEC, which has created a new set of rivalries from when I attended A&M. In my day, the biggest game of the year was the final season game against the University of Texas Longhorns.

Miguel and I met for lunch at Papa's Seafood on I-45. I had a plate of fried oysters with French fries. Miguel said, "Go ahead and eat all of that fried food. I'm a trained medic. I'll keep you alive until the ambulance arrives."

I said, "I feel better now. The chest pains have almost subsided. I think I'll order a banana split for dessert."

I was preparing the bill to give to Karen and wanted to be sure to include all the expenses that Miguel had incurred during our time working together. Miguel, on the other hand, was totally cavalier about his expenses and said, "Don't worry about it. We nailed some bad guys and thwarted a terrorist plot, that is its own reward."

I thanked Miguel for all the help. He said, "Call me anytime, I consider it my duty to bail out Army Rangers when they get over their heads in shit."

I couldn't let that one pass, "You've got it backwards, the truth is that the Rangers are always there with the firepower to bail out you squids when the shit hits the fan."

We both laughed.

Chapter 39

The weather was perfect. There wasn't a cloud in the sky and the temperature was almost ninety degrees when Pal and I left the apartment and headed for College Station. The traffic was light as we drove up Highway 290. When we got to Hempstead, we took a right turn on Highway 6. Thirty minutes later we were approaching College Station. You knew it was College Station because Kyle Field, the Texas A&M football stadium, was visible for miles before you arrived.

Actually, College Station and Bryan, Texas were one continuous city. Except for the signs that told you when you left one and entered the other, you would never know.

My mom and dad lived in a relatively new community called Traditions. It was located near Easterwood Airport that served the Bryan-College Station area. It was a five-minute drive from the A&M campus. Most of the families living there were former Aggies that enjoyed the small-town friendliness and, most importantly, easy access to athletic events. Although football was still king, A&M had developed its other programs to where they were nationally competitive. This was especially true with its women's teams.

As we pulled into the driveway, the whole family came out to meet us. My sister, Jane, and her husband, Tom, and four-year-old Tom Junior had already arrived. As I opened the driver's door, Pal bounded over me and jumped out of the truck. He loved kids and made a beeline for Tom Junior with his tail going a mile a minute. There were hugs and kisses all around.

We spent the next two hours talking about family stuff and reminiscing about growing up in places like Schweinfurt, Germany, Fort Bragg, North Carolina, Leavenworth, Kansas and Washington, D.C.. Jane and her husband, Tom, were both junior partners in a private equity firm in Houston that specialized in energy. They were all interested in my job as a PI and especially my latest mission. I gave them a vanilla version of my trip to Lebanon and Mexico. I left out all the dangerous and exciting stuff.

Fortunately, Mom called everyone to dinner just as Jane was asking some probing questions about what had happened in Beirut. Tom Junior and Pal heard the call and came in from outside where they had been playing fetch for the last hour. Pal had gotten his exercise for the day.

My mom isn't the greatest cook, but this meal was the exception. I thought she had had it catered when I came into the dining room. A large roasted turkey was on the table, surrounded by bowls of dressing, cranberry sauce, creamed spinach and mashed potatoes.

All I could say when I saw it was, "Wow, this is terrific!"

My dad said, "Yeah, and it isn't even Thanksgiving."

Mom said, "It's in honor of the return of the prodigal son," as she glanced at me, "I know this is your favorite meal."

Rather than saying something clever, I just said, "Thanks, Mom."

We all enjoyed the meal immensely, especially me. The conversation was pleasant. Thankfully, no one brought up Lebanon or Mexico. Instead, we listened to Jane and Tom talk about oil and gas. They were working on a deal involving the construction of a liquid natural gas export project to be built on the Texas coast that would sell Texas gas to buyers in Asia. I wondered how Jane and Tom could work together. Both were extremely competitive. Jane had an MBA from Rice, Tom from Harvard.

After dinner, we all sat around and listened to Dad talk about the attributes of the A&M football coach and his prediction that they would win the SEC next season. I chimed in. "You better figure out how to beat Alabama."

He responded, "Hey, we beat them our first year in the SEC."

I said, "Sure, Dad, but what happened the next two years?"

"Well son, we won't talk about those games. I can't believe that I actually flew up to Tuscaloosa for that game. You have to hand it to Alabama, that place knows something about football. That stadium is ringed with flags commemorating national championships."

I noticed Jane rolling her eyes, so I changed the subject, "How about those Astros?"

Jane said, "Tom Junior has a soccer game in the morning, so we better get going."

It was hugs and kisses all around again. Jane, Tom and Tom Junior piled in their Land Rover. Everybody waved as they drove off. They seemed very happy. It made me wonder what it would be like to settle down and have a family. Maybe later, for now I was enjoying my new career as a gumshoe. At the advanced age of thirty, I decided I still had time to ponder the family scene. For now I was content to be a bachelor.

I said, "I better get on the road too."

Mom had already gone into the house. Dad said, "You're not going anywhere until you tell me what really happened in Lebanon and Mexico. My bullshit detector still works fine, thank you."

"Dad, you know me too well." I gave him a full blow-by-blow account of what had happened while we were together on the porch.

He said, "That's quite a story, a real adventure for sure. I read about a car chase and shoot out in Houston, but there was no mention of captured missiles or a terrorist plot."

"I'm sure the FBI wants to keep a lid on it for a couple of reasons. There are still people like the dark-haired woman at large. I'm sure they don't want it publicized that they failed to stop the Mercedes at the border."

Mom came to the door and asked, "What are you two plotting out here. You can come in now, since I alone have cleaned up and loaded the dishwasher."

I said, "You are a master of guilt, Mom."

She replied, "Yes, I am. Unfortunately it no longer works on your father."

Dad grinned.

I thanked Mom for a wonderful dinner. I had to wake up Pal who was sound asleep in the living room. He was no doubt recovering from the ball game with Tom Junior. As we drove off, my cell phone rang. It was Captain Fortis. His first words were, "Amigo, we've got a problem."

Chapter 40

Fortis said that the coroner could only identify one of the two bodies from the shootout. One was a Mexican national known to be associated with the Zetas. He had previously been a member of El Chapo's Sinaloa Cartel before joining the Zetas. He was carrying a stolen passport, but we had the prints on file. "The other guy, who we think is Amir Lahoud, has no fingerprints. He was carrying Lahoud's passport, and he fits the description, but this print thing is weird. We have Lahoud's prints, but of course, there isn't a match. The coroner says that the prints had been removed surgically very recently."

He went on to say that the coroner was trying to contact Karen to get a positive ID on Amir. He gave me the number for the coroner.

I called Karen and told her about the fingerprints and that the coroner wanted her to make a positive identification. She said she would call right away. She asked me to go with her to identify Amir's body. I said I would.

Karen said she and Thomas were packed and ready to come home. She knew it was time to put Amir's affairs in order. She also told me to write up my invoice and she would give me a check. I told her I was truly sorry it had worked out this way.

It was four in the afternoon the following day when Karen called and asked me to meet her at the coroner's office in downtown Houston. She gave me the address and asked me to meet her there in an hour. The traffic was heavy, but I managed to arrive almost on time.

When they rolled the body out, it was disfigured by a gunshot wound to the forehead. Karen drew back and grabbed my arm when they uncovered the body and didn't want to look. I put my arm around her, and we moved closer to the body. Tears were running down her cheeks. Then something amazing happened. Karen said, "That's not Amir."

I said, "Are you sure? There has been a lot of damage from the bullet."

She responded, "I'm sure. Amir has a small mole on his left cheek. It's not him."

The coroner asked if he could have the name of Amir's dentist. She gave it to him.

The impact of Karen's claim that this was not Amir's body was just beginning to register in my mind. If this wasn't Amir, who was it? More importantly, where the hell was Amir? My thoughts immediately turned to the dark-haired woman. She was the key to this puzzle or at least the only one I could think of at the moment.

Karen was a basket case. The events were an emotional rollercoaster for her. First her husband was missing and probably having an affair, then he was dead, and now he was missing again.

I followed Karen home. She had dropped Thomas off at a friend's house on the way to the coroner. I checked the house carefully. Everything seemed to be in order. There were several messages on the answering machine, but nothing of substance.

No message from Amir. We went together to pick up Thomas, who was elated to hear that his father was not in the Houston morgue.

I drove Karen and Thomas home. When we arrived, Karen asked, "Would you like to stay for dinner? It won't be anything fancy."

I said, "Thanks, that would be great. It would give us a chance to talk about what had happened and try to figure out what we should do next now that we know that Amir is alive." I would have said maybe he's alive, but Thomas was listening to every word.

Since I had no idea what was going on at this point, except that Amir was still missing, I told Karen and Thomas that I would feel better if they stayed somewhere else until things became more clear.

Karen asked, "John, I am so confused and scared. Thomas and I can leave tomorrow, but would you stay with us tonight?"

"Sure." What else could I say?

Karen served us toasted cheese sandwiches and tomato soup. Thomas wanted a hamburger. I secretly agreed with him. After we ate, Karen cleared the table. Thomas headed into the den saying he was going to watch TV. I helped Karen, then looked in on Thomas. He was watching TV, using his I-Pad and texting someone – all at the same time. Typical kid.

Karen and I sat down in the living room. I said, "Tell me about Amir. I've been following him through three countries, and I haven't a clue as to what kind of a person he is."

Karen responded, "John, I am beginning to wonder if I even know him. He is an excellent provider and a good father. I frankly don't give him high marks as a husband, especially during the last few years. It is hard to know what Amir is thinking."

"What about his politics? Could he be part of a terrorist cell?"

She replied, "Amir is a devout Muslim, but I can't imagine that he would be a crazy radical. He has always complained about our involvement in Iraq and Afghanistan, but so have a lot of other people. He is a tolerant man. He agreed when I wanted to give our son a Christian name. An extremist would have never done that."

I said, "I agree, just because Amir is Muslim doesn't mean he is a terrorist. I've made some very good friends in both Iraq and Afghanistan who are Muslims. They are decent peace-loving people. The Islamic terrorists have corrupted the religion. Evil people have used religion to justify evil actions for centuries."

Karen said, "Amir is in trouble. I know it. Please try to help him."

I said I would. Karen told Thomas to go to bed. She led me to the guest room. It was filled with expensive Ethan Allen furniture. I decided I could get used to this lifestyle. I undressed, took a shower and climbed into bed.

I couldn't sleep. I kept thinking about what had happened in Beirut. If only I had spoken to Amir when he answered the phone in the hotel. Maybe I could have convinced him to come back to Houston with me. If I had gone to his room, maybe it would have changed everything that had happened.

I realized that dwelling on what might have happened if I had done something different was totally unproductive. What was important was to map out a plan for the future. I knew that Karen wanted me to continue the hunt for Amir and I had agreed.

I decided that I needed to do some real systematic investigating. I was in a totally reactive mode. I needed to take the initiative and find out everything possible about Amir. I knew very little about him and his business. That was going to change. With that thought in mind, I drifted off to sleep.

Chapter 40

It was two o'clock when I heard a light tapping on the guest room door where I was sleeping. Karen looked in and asked if she could come in. I nodded, sat up and turned on the lamp next to the bed. She came over and sat on the edge of the bed. She was wearing one of those bathrobes that you find at the Ritz or Four Seasons. When she sat down on the edge of the bed, her bathrobe parted showing her well-shaped legs.

"John, I can't sleep. I'm a wreck. Tell me what to do."

"Karen, all you can do at this point is take care of Thomas and yourself. In the morning, I want you to go somewhere safe, maybe a spa in San Antonio or Phoenix. I also want you to call Amir's office and see if they have heard from him. Tell them to allow me to go through all of Amir's files."

"Okay, but will you be able to find him?" she asked as tears welled up in her eyes.

"Yes, Karen, I will find him."

"Oh thank you." Then she hesitated and said, "Can I stay here with you for a while, John?"

I felt a surge inside of me and said, "Sure."

Karen slipped out of her robe, revealing rather sexy pajamas, and climbed into bed. After a few minutes, she snuggled up to me and put one leg over mine. I'm a tough guy, but there are limits to my willpower.

I managed to get control and said to Karen, "You are a beautiful woman, but I don't want us to do something we may both regret."

I rolled over turning my back to Karen.

She whispered in my ear, "You're an honorable man, John Remington."

Karen spooned and immediately fell asleep. I, on the other hand, couldn't sleep thinking about what I had just done or not done.

When I woke up at seven, Karen was gone. I could hear her talking to Thomas about the need to go somewhere for another week or so. They were talking about various places to go.

We all ate breakfast together. Karen and Thomas had not completely unpacked from the trip to Dallas and Arkansas so getting ready for another trip was quick and easy. They decided to go to a fancy resort and spa near Austin. As before, I followed them northwest on Highway 290 to the cutoff for Prairie View, Texas, the home of Prairie View A&M University. By that time I was certain that no one was trying to follow them, and I turned around.

On my way back, I tried to reach both Fortis and Roberts on my cell. I left voice messages for both of them. I went directly to Amir's office. I pulled into the spot where Amir had parked when I first started following him several weeks earlier. I walked into the office, which consisted of a receptionist desk, a well-appointed conference room and several offices. A woman in her late fifties was at the reception desk. I introduced myself. She said, "Oh, Mister Remington, I'm Kirsten Burrows, the office manager here. Karen called earlier and said you would be coming by and to make everything available to you. You can use the conference room or Amir's office, whichever you prefer."

"Thanks, Kirsten. I'll use Amir's office. I would like to talk to each of the people working here and see if we can find Amir. Can you arrange that?"

"Of course, Mister Remington, who would you like to see first?"

"You."

I spent the next thirty minutes with Kirsten. She had worked for Amir for over ten years. She described him as a great boss, although very thorough and meticulous. She had no idea where he was and had heard nothing from him or anyone else since he left her a voice message the day he left town. Just as I finished talking to Kirsten, my cell phone buzzed. It was Fortis.

I asked, "How's your officer?"

"Doc says he'll live. He lost his spleen and will have a hell of a scar on his neck, but all and all, he was pretty lucky. He's a good guy, fifteen years on the force, wife and two kids. Thank Miguel again for me."

"Good to hear, what about the bad guys?"

"They're both dead."

I said, "Thanks Captain Obvious, I knew that. What about who they are and what was in that car?"

The FBI is being very secretive about all of that, but I got a guy working with them. So you didn't hear any of this from me, capiche?"

"Roger that."

"Both were carrying American passports. One was using Amir's, but the doc says the dental records don't match. They have no idea who he really is. The other guy is a Mexican named Manuel Sanchez, but he was using the passport of a guy named George Villa, whose last address was in the apartment on the sixth floor that you found. Sanchez also had a Mexican driver's license with an address in Mexico City. Feds have been all over that apartment and are trying to figure it all out."

"What about the dark-haired woman?"

Fortis said, "No sign of her. The Feds went into every apartment but found nothing. She's a mystery."

"What about the car? It looked like surface to air missiles in one of the compartments, that's a really big deal."

"Tip of the iceberg, Ranger. There were six Strelas missiles, six RPG7 launchers and thirty rockets and a 40-pound shaped charge. There were also a shitload of hand grenades, six MP5s and enough nine-millimeter ammo to take over a small country. They really had that car loaded."

"Lucky that the crash didn't set any of that stuff off. It's a tribute to how military gear is made," I said. "I guess we know what Amir and his buddies were talking about when they said it was a dangerous shipment."

Fortis asked, "What are you and your squid friend going to do now?"

"Good question. I'm still on the job with the mission to find Amir. The fucking guy could be anywhere. Got any ideas?"

"No, not really. Just some advice for you, watch your ass. Roberts is under the gun, so don't cross him. I'll let you know if something more develops."

I thanked the Captain and called Roberts again. No answer, just his voice mail. I told him that Karen and Thomas were in hiding. If he needed to talk to them, give me a call and I would give him the location.

I interviewed the bookkeeper next. His name was Saif Suleman and like the other man in the office, he was Amir's cousin. Like Kirsten, he had no idea where Amir was or why he left in such a hurry. He was very surprised to hear that Amir had gone to Lebanon without telling either him or Habib, the other cousin. He showed me all of the recent transactions and all of the accounts. Amir's little company had excellent cash flow. It made me wonder why he would get tangled up in what was obviously a terrorist plan.

The last person I interviewed was Habib Lahoud. Keeping business in the family was very much of an Arab way of doing things. The Lebanese in particular had a reputation as excellent businessmen. They were often described as traders all over the world. Habib, like Kirsten and Saif, claimed to know nothing of Amir's whereabouts. However, I had a feeling Habib knew more than he was saying. He said that Amir had left without telling him anything.

I said, "Habib, I am a trained interrogator. You are not being honest with me. I can make things very difficult for you given what has happened recently. The FBI is involved in Amir's disappearance, and you could be in a lot of trouble if I point them in your direction. Do you have any idea why Amir would travel to Beirut?"

"Mister Remington, I really do not know where he is or why he might go there. There is one thing that might be important. I don't know. I received a call from my mother, Amir's aunt, two days after Amir left. Of course, I had no idea that he had gone to Lebanon. My mother told me that she had just spoken to her sister, Amir's mother, and she seemed very afraid of something."

"Did she mention Amir?"

"No, she said she asked her sister what was wrong, but she wouldn't tell her anything."

"Okay, Habib. Now I believe you. I want you to call your mother and see if she knows anything else. I also want the addresses and phone numbers of your mother and Amir's mother." I gave him my card.

"Mister Remington, I will do it, but please be careful. Lebanon can be dangerous, and I don't want anything to happen to my family back there."

I agreed.

Before I left the office, I went through Amir's desk and files. I looked under his desk and checked for hidden panels. I found nothing. I called Miguel and he agreed to meet me for dinner at Papa's on Westheimer Road at eight o'clock. I had an idea.

Chapter 41

I arrived at the restaurant first. It was packed with young business types. There was a twenty-minute wait, so I sat at the bar and waited for Miguel. He strolled in just as the hostess was calling my name.

"Your timing is impeccable as usual. I don't mind being your point man."

Miguel's response was predictable, "As it should be, didn't you always tell me that Rangers lead the way."

"I guess you've got me there, but I thought restaurants were an exception."

"Nope."

I told Miguel everything that Fortis had told me as well as my conversation with Habib.

He said, "You're going back to Lebanon, aren't you?"

"How the hell did you know what I was thinking? Yes, as a matter of fact I am. I'm beginning to believe that Amir never left Beirut. The real question for me is whether Amir is a good guy or a bad guy. I was convinced that he had gone to the dark side until we found out he wasn't in that car."

Miguel responded, "You want company?"

"Sure, it's good to have a squid following in support,"

"Fuck you, grunt. Okay, I'll go. Somebody needs to be around to save your ass."

We both had ten-ounce filets rare with loaded baked potatoes. It was a great meal topped off with key lime pie, a restaurant specialty.

On the way home, I called Karen. She had made it safely to the resort and said Thomas was out on the driving range. I told her about my plan, including that Miguel was going with me to Beirut. She agreed immediately.

I picked up Pal and told Mary that I would be leaving again tomorrow to return to Beirut. She frowned and said, "John, you be careful. It's dangerous over there and I don't want Pal to be an orphan."

"No worries, I've appointed you as his legal guardian in my will."

She said, "I'm serious, John. Please be extra careful. Is Miguel going with you?"

When I told her he was going, she gave a sigh of relief and said, "Well, I feel a little better now. Miguel is a SEAL, isn't he?"

"Yes, Mary. But he is a good guy in spite of it. What is all this hype about SEALs? They must have a great public relations department, even better than the Marines."

She laughed.

I said good night. Pal and I went upstairs. I called my dad and told him what had happened and that I was going back to Lebanon to find Amir. He said, "Be careful, Son. My experience in that part of the world is that things are rarely as they seem. One of my best friends was an Egyptian Army general who commanded a tank division. He once told me, 'Arabs are warm and friendly people as a rule, but they have a cultural inclination to not give you the whole story. Being devious is often considered an attribute.'"

"Thanks for the advice, Dad. I'll definitely keep that in mind. Please don't mention where I'm going to Mom. I know how she worries."

He assured me that he would keep our conversation between us. His last words were, "Be safe."

Chapter 42

I was awake at six. My mind was racing. I thought about how to approach Amir's relatives in Lebanon, since they were my best and probably my only lead there. I had the same feeling that I often recall having before kicking off a new combat operation that you knew was going to be dicey.

Pal and I did our standard five-mile run to and from Memorial Park. It might be my last decent chance to exercise for the next week. Body maintenance was something I learned to respect as a Ranger. Do it whenever you can, because there will be times when it will save your life. There will also be times when you won't be able to do it. I took a shower and packed my bag for the trip. Pal and I went down to the office to make final preparations.

I made reservations for Miguel and myself on the same Qatar flights I had taken previously. I called Habib who told me that he had called his mother repeatedly, but no one had answered. He said he would keep trying. He gave me his mother's phone number and address but did not have the contact information for Amir's mother. I told him to keep trying and text me with the number and address when he got them.

Miguel and I met at the airline's lounge in Terminal B at Bush Intercontinental Airport. We were both traveling light with only a carry-on bag. Miguel asked, "What about weapons? Are we able to get some when we arrive?"

I said, "I'm sure we'll find some."

Miguel responded, "Hmm, that doesn't sound very definitive. What do you have in mind?"

"Between my contact at the Embassy and my buddy, Ahmed, we'll get some guns, trust me."

Miguel said, "Famous last words."

The in-bound flight was late, which delayed our takeoff by about an hour. It was not a problem because we had several hours to layover in Doha.

I had called Major Tom Williamson before we took off and gave him a quick rundown on what had occurred. I told him that Miguel and I were coming to Beirut to find Amir. I told him when we were arriving and that we were staying at the Hilton again. He offered a car, but I told him that Ahmed was scheduled to pick us up at the airport. We agreed to meet for breakfast after we arrived.

The flight to Doha seemed to take longer this time. I managed to sleep some but kept waking up thinking about Amir and wondering how we were going to find him. Miguel, on the other hand, probably logged a good ten hours of solid sleep after we took off. In fact, I think he was asleep *before* we took off.

Although we were a few minutes late arriving in Doha, we easily made our connection to Beirut. As expected, Ahmed was standing outside the secure area when we cleared customs.

"Mister John, it is so good to see you. How was your flight? Let me take your bag."

"Thanks, Ahmed. The flight was fine. Let's go straight to the hotel. We can talk on the way about what has happened since I left."

I introduced Miguel to Ahmed, and we drove to the Hilton. It had been several years since Miguel had been in Lebanon. He was amazed at the changes that had occurred, especially the construction that was ongoing.

The clerk at the desk said, "Mr. Remington, welcome back. We have upgraded you into a suite. I hope you like it."

Miguel grumbled, "Figures. They probably have me in a broom closet."

The clerk heard him and said, "Oh no, Mister Monterossa, we have you in a suite just like Mister Remington." Miguel smiled.

After we checked in, I called Major Williamson's direct line. He answered on the first ring. I said, "Hi Tom, John Remington. I'm back and I brought a buddy with me that is no stranger to trouble."

Williamson said, "I hope this trip is quieter than your last one. From some of the reports our FBI rep has been getting, trouble seems to follow you around. How long will you be here?"

I replied, "Hopefully not too long. I have some leads to follow up that should shed some light on what my target has been doing and what might be next."

Tom said, "You guys get some sleep and I'll meet you at eight o'clock in the morning."

I said, "Roger that."

I called Miguel and told him about the meeting with Major Williamson in the morning.

I took a long shower and climbed into bed. I wasn't usually bothered by changes in time zones. I had always said that if you didn't dwell on them, they wouldn't be a problem. However, I had a difficult time going to sleep. I looked around the hotel room and wondered what I would do if there was an attack on the hotel. I recalled being in Amman, Jordan when a truck bomb hit my hotel, but no one tried to take over the hotel. I concluded that since I was on the tenth floor, jumping out of the window was not an option. My only chance was to ambush whoever came into my room first, disarm him and use the weapon against the rest. It was a weak plan at best, especially if the attackers had their act together. I drifted off having successfully defeated the attackers in my mind. Fortunately, it was a quiet night and the whole thing was theoretical.

Chapter 43

Williamson met us in the breakfast room of the Hilton, the same place I had seen Amir with the dark-haired woman and the two other men. He already knew a good bit of what occurred in Houston, which likely came through the FBI representative at the Embassy. We went over all the details and then focused in on what Habib had told me regarding his mother and her conversation with Amir's mother. Williamson wrote down the address and phone number of Habib's mother. He said he would be back to me in a few hours.

Miguel and I finished breakfast. I called Ahmed and asked him to meet us in the lobby as soon as possible. Ten minutes later, Ahmed called and said he was there. Miguel, Ahmed and I found three comfortable chairs in a quiet corner of the lobby. I told Ahmed that we needed to visit Habib's mother and showed him the address. Ahmed explained that the address was actually in a small village on the outskirts of Beirut.

I asked, "Ahmed, how long will it take to get there?"

"Depending on the traffic, Mister John, we should be there in thirty minutes unless we go during rush hour."

"What about security, is it in a safe area?"

"It is not a bad area, but things can happen quickly here. I would recommend we bring some type of security with us."

"Do you know anyone who could provide security, someone we can really trust?

"I have an uncle who owns a small security company. I would trust him with my life."

I said, "Maybe you will have to." It was a joke, but nobody laughed.

Ahmed called his uncle. Thirty minutes later his uncle, Saif, arrived at the hotel. Saif spoke limited English, but we were able to communicate pretty well. He took us out to the parking area in front of the hotel. There were three of his men there alongside an old grey Toyota Land cruiser. None of the men spoke English. Miguel looked inside the vehicle. There were three AK47s and twenty thirty-round magazines.

We agreed on a price for the security team and two handguns for us, military model 9-millimeter Berettas with four magazines each. Saif said, "Try not to shoot anybody, let my guys do it. I'm not supposed to give clients weapons."

We loaded up in the two vehicles. Miguel and I rode in Ahmed's car, while Saif's team followed in the Toyota. Ahmed gave a heshma or head scarf to Miguel and me and suggested we also wear sunglasses. The ride to Habib's mother's house was uneventful. It was actually quite scenic and a good chance to see part of Beirut. Miguel had been in Beirut on a mission during his SEAL days.

We started formulating a plan for when we arrived at the house. Ahmed thought it best to let him go to the door first. We didn't know if Habib's mother spoke any English.

The house was larger than I had expected. A six-foot wall with an iron gate in front surrounded it. Ahmed went to the gate and rang the bell while Miguel and I stayed in the car. A man dressed in a dishdasha, or traditional dress came to the gate. Ahmed exchanged words with him. He left and a few minutes later returned with a woman that looked to be in her sixties. After a brief exchange with her, Ahmed motioned for us to come. We went through the gate and into the house. It was very clean and neat with old rugs and furniture. Ahmed introduced everyone. Habib's mother's name was Hala and her husband's name was Nader.

She brought us sweet tea and small cookies. Her English was fair. She told us that she had made several visits to Houston to visit Habib. I told her about my conversation with Habib and that we had been hired to find Amir. The last he had been seen was two weeks before at the Hilton here in Beirut. I told her that there was great concern for his safety. I didn't mention the events in Mexico or what just occurred in Houston with Amir's car.

She told me that it had been nearly two weeks since she had talked to her sister, Amir's mother, and was very concerned as well. She said that during their last call, she thought her sister sounded as though there was something wrong, but she claimed everything was fine when asked several times. Hala said she had gone to her sister's home twice and tried to call her every day, but no one answered. She said she was very close to her sister and that she was sure that something was wrong.

I asked, "Is it possible she has gone on a trip, maybe a vacation?"

"My sister and I share everything. She would never leave without telling me where she was going and when she would be back."

I said, "Please try to call now." There was no answer.

I asked, "Have you called the police?"

She responded, "No, I keep hoping that she will call. I don't trust the police here.

Hala gave us the address and phone number for her sister. She also gave us the phone and address of Amir's brother, Bashir, who lived in Tyre, a Lebanese city in the south along the coast near the border with Israel. I left her my card, as did Ahmed, and told her to please call me immediately if anything new developed. She agreed.

Chapter 44

Ahmed said that it would take about forty minutes to get to Amir's mother's house. We arrived there without incident. It was similar to the Hala's home with a high stone wall around it. We followed the same plan as before, with Ahmed ringing the bell. However, this time there was no response. The walls were linked to similar houses on each side of the mother's home. Ahmed went to the neighbors on each side. In both cases, they said that they had not seen anyone in or around the house for some time. They said that was unusual, except when they were traveling out of the country.

Miguel and I went over the wall and into a small garden by the front door. The front door was unlocked. We went in and did a standard clearing of each room. There was no one in the house and there was no sign of foul play. The only thing that seemed strange was the fact that the front door had not been locked. It looked like another dead end.

When we got back into the car Miguel said, "Okay, Ranger John, what's the plan now?"

"I don't have one."

"Oh great!"

I said, "Maybe we should call Amir's brother in Tyre."

Miguel said, "Tyre, that's just where I want to go. Maybe we can ask Hezbollah to help us while we're there."

I dialed the number we received from Hala for her Amir's brother. When a man answered, I handed the cell phone to Ahmed. He said he needed to talk to Bashir. The man said that Bashir was not there and hung up. Ahmed said, "Whoever that man was, he was not friendly. What do you want to do now, Mister John?"

"Let's go back to the hotel, Ahmed. We need a new plan."

The traffic was very heavy in the evening. It took us over an hour to get back to the hotel. During that time, I spoke to Major Williamson. I told him everything that had happened since we met for breakfast that morning. He agreed to meet us at eight for dinner back at the Hilton.

When we arrived back at the hotel, I told Ahmed we would not need him or the team until the next day. I told him to have everyone back at seven-thirty in the morning with full tanks of gas in each vehicle.

We had nearly an hour before dinner. Miguel and I went back to our rooms to wait. I used the time to check in with key people back in Houston. I called Karen and told her everything that had happened and that costs were mounting. She said, "John, I need to know what has happened to Amir. I will spend whatever is needed to find him."

I said, "Alright, we'll stay on it. I'll keep you posted."

Next, I called Captain Fortis. "How's it going, Cap?"

He said, "Well, well, if it isn't the Lebanese version of Lawrence of Arabia. I've decided that I like it better when you and your squid friend are out of town. There's no kidnappings or terrorists. It's a great chance for me to do what the City of

Houston pays me to do. If you want something, the answer is no."

I said, "You've hurt my feelings. I was actually calling to wish you a happy birthday."

"Sorry asshole, it's not my birthday."

I said, "Anniversary?"

"No."

"Okay, did you identify the dead man that was carrying Amir's passport?"

"No."

I said, "Nice talking to you."

Fortis said, "Seriously, keep checking in with me and stay safe over there, Ranger."

Lastly, I called Special Agent Roberts. This time he answered. I briefed him on what occurred since the last time we had been together in Houston.

He listened. Then he said, "I don't have anything new that I can share with you. Frankly, at this point the less I share with you the more likely you and your friends will not muck up my case. Let me remind you one more time, this is FBI business. It's not for amateurs." He hung up. Once again, I concluded that Roberts was an asshole. On fact, I upgraded him to a flaming asshole.

At eight sharp, I walked into the restaurant. Miguel and Williamson were already there and engaged in conversation. We feasted on the buffet, which had the full range of Lebanese cuisines. I had red lentil soup, lamb kabobs, hummus and flat bread, with baklava for dessert.

After dinner, we talked about what to do next. Major Williamson said that there was some intelligence based on local intercepts that related to the captured shipment in Houston. He said there was nothing that he considered "actionable." I told him that we were planning to drive to Tyre tomorrow and see what was going on with Amir's brother, Bashir. Williamson said he would like to go with us but would have to check with the Defense Attaché. We agreed to meet at the hotel at seven-thirty if he was able to come along.

Chapter 45

At seven in the morning, Major Williamson called and said that he did not have clearance to go with us to Tyre. He said that the Defense Attaché had disapproved his request. Williamson also quoted his boss as saying, “Tell your buddies that going down there is fucking nuts.”

Williamson then said, “I’ve given you the message. I know you are going anyway, so keep me in the loop and I’ll do what I can to help you.”

I thanked him and went down to meet Miguel for breakfast. He was not surprised to hear that the Embassy had denied Williamson’s request and said, “First rule of the bureaucracy is to cover your ass.”

While we were enjoying a combination of Lebanese food and good old American pancakes and eggs, Ahmed came into the dining room. Miguel and I laughed when he said in his distinct Arabic accent, “Okay boys, let’s rock and roll!”

We checked the security team thoroughly and found them ready. Their weapons were clean, and their magazines were in the vests that each man was wearing. This was a good indicator because the norm in the Middle East region is for militias to carry just an AK with a magazine in the weapon and nothing more. The exception being professional military units like those found in Jordan, Turkey and occasionally in Iraq and Syria. The team also had handheld radios with them.

We headed south out of Beirut. The morning traffic was heavy. I was amazed at the amount of construction going on in the city. Ahmed explained that there continued to be a great deal of high-rise apartments under construction. He said that there were many Lebanese living all over the world, but they wanted to have a place to come back to in Lebanon. It was also a place where wealthy families from throughout the Arab world wanted to have an apartment where they could spend vacations in a more free and secular environment.

It was a warm summer day without a cloud in the sky. As we traveled south out of Beirut, the traffic began to thin out. There was one military checkpoint, but we were waived through without incident. Ahmed's calls on his cell phone to Amir's brother all went unanswered.

We decided to drive by the house before stopping to see if there was any unusual activity. The house was located on an unpaved road. Like the houses we visited in Beirut, it was large with a high wall on all sides. I noticed that there was man sitting at the corner of the flat roof on the house watching the street below. Given the angle looking up, it was impossible to tell if he was armed. My assumption was that he most likely was and he was keeping the weapon where it couldn't be observed.

I had an uneasy feeling about the situation. We drove to a location several blocks away and got the whole team together. Our options included keeping the house under observation and waiting, simply going to the door and asking for Bashir, or actively trying to get more information on what was going on in the house. We decided on the last option. Ahmed would go to a neighbor's house and see what he could find out.

Ahmed rode in one of the Toyotas to the house next door to Bashir's. He went to the gate and rang the bell. After an exchange, an older man in his late sixties wearing a traditional dishdasha came to the gate. Ahmed obviously used his friendly approach because the man invited him into the house. We waited. Ahmed finally emerged from the house after nearly an hour and returned to our rendezvous location several blocks from the house.

Ahmed reported that the neighbor knew Bashir very well. He said that something very strange had been going on at the house. He had not actually seen Bashir for over two weeks, which he said was very unusual. He said it was normal for him and Bashir to have tea together several times a week. Ahmed said he asked the neighbor if there had been any unusual activity at Bashir's house. The neighbor said that he had only noticed activity twice, both times at night. Two SUVs had arrived and left at about midnight, but he had no idea who was in them or where they were going. He told us that he had never seen the vehicles before at Bashir's house. When asked about the man on the roof, the neighbor said he had not seen him.

Like every other event in this case, there was no clear-cut situation or solution. I suspected foul play, but it was impossible to know without getting into that house. Ahmed suggested that he go up to the house and ask for Bashir. That at least would give us some idea as to what was going on at the house. I reluctantly agreed.

Ahmed drove up to the house and went to the gate. He thought it best if he went alone this time. We watched from the end of the block as he rang the bell. The gate opened and there was a brief dialogue with a young, bearded man. Ahmed entered and was out of sight.

We waited. I began to worry after thirty minutes. After an hour, I really began to worry. After three hours, I concluded that we now had another missing person in this case.

Chapter 46

What should we do now? Miguel and I decided to call Major Williamson and let him know what had happened. He listened intently, and then said, "This has the makings of a real disaster. The last thing I want to do is report that you guys have been taken hostage in Tyre. No, the worst thing would be reporting that you both had been killed in Tyre."

I said, "Well, we'll try to avoid both those reports. We'll try to get some help from the local cops."

We found a local police station. It was a small, one-story building that had seen better days. We sent the leader of the security team in to report that their Lebanese client had gone into the house and had not come out and failed to answer his cell phone. His mission was to have them go to the house and check it out.

After about fifteen minutes, the team leader came out shaking his head. He spoke enough English to tell us that the police were not going to get involved. He made it clear that the police were afraid to confront a possible kidnapping situation.

We devised a simple plan. Miguel and I would wait until dark before scaling the wall. At the same time, the security team would go to the gate and tell whoever answered that they were looking for Ahmed who had come there earlier. They were not to be confrontational but were to create enough of a distraction to allow Miguel and I to enter the compound unnoticed.

The team was reluctant to give Miguel and I two of the AKs, but finally agreed. We donned their ammo vests and darkened our faces as we waited for night. Ideally, we would have preferred to go in at three o'clock in the morning but decided that the benefit of having the security team come to the gate at a reasonable hour in the evening as a diversion outweighed the benefits of waiting.

By nine o'clock it was totally dark. Miguel and crept to the rear of the house. At exactly ten after nine, the team rang the bell. At the same time, Miguel boosted me up on the wall. There was imbedded glass on the top of the wall. We had brought a piece of canvas to deal with that possibility. I threw it over the glass and lay on the top of the wall and pulled Miguel up. Within ten seconds we were in the compound, apparently undetected. We moved toward the front of the house where we could hear the conversation between the team and the man who had come to the gate. He had not opened the gate and it was clear that he did not intend to do so.

The windows on the house were high, which meant Miguel and I had to use a similar technique to boost each other up to see in. After checking all the windows on the first floor, we determined that there five men in the living room. They were all looking out the window at the dialogue going on between their man at the gate and our team. Each of them was holding an AK47. We assumed there was still a sentry on the roof. Therefore, we knew that there were at least seven men at the house counting the one that was still at the gate. There was no way to know if there were more people upstairs.

We went to the rear of the house and checked the door. It was locked. We went to a window adjacent to the door. Miguel boosted me up and I was able to raise the window. He handed me both AKs and I pulled him up. We were in the kitchen. There was a light on in the hallway leading to the front of the house. There was a stairwell to the right that went upstairs and another to the left that went into the basement. I waited while Miguel went upstairs. In a few minutes, he came back and said there was no one upstairs. He stayed by the staircase while I went down into the basement. I needed the flashlight to see. At the bottom of the stairs, there was another door to the right. It was locked with a padlock. I put my ear to the door but could hear nothing. It was a heavy steel door. I rapped lightly on the door and put my ear to the door again. I could hear movement inside.

I scanned the basement for something that I could use to break the padlock. I could use the barrel of the AK but was loathed to do that. I went back upstairs and told Miguel what I had found. Miguel said, "Wait here." He crept up the stairs and disappeared.

A few minutes later, he was back with another AK, which I was able to use to break the padlock. I shined the light inside. There were two men bound with their heads covered by canvas sacks. I recognized Ahmed by his clothes. I quickly untied him and took a gag that had been stuffed into his mouth. He hugged me. I did the same for the other man. It was not Amir. He told me his name was Bashir, Amir's brother. He hugged me too.

As we started up the stairs, I heard yelling in Arabic followed by the combined fire of multiple weapons. They were loud and I recognized them as AKs. I ran to the top of the stairs and motioned for Ahmed and Bashir to stop. Miguel was in the stairwell going upstairs. One of the kidnappers lay dead a few feet from Miguel. A gun battle was raging down the hallway leading to the living room. There was great deal of yelling coming from the living room.

The firing subsided enough for me to tell Miguel that we needed to watch form them coming around the house and outflanking us, and to watch the roof. Miguel said not to worry about the roof. I knew immediately where he had gotten the AK that I had used to break the padlock.

The kidnappers did not yet know I was on the other side of the hallway. I motioned for Ahmed and Bashir to come to where I was at the top of the stairs.

I motioned to Miguel to move on three to the back door. He knew I would lay down suppressive fire to cover his move. I counted with my fingers. On three, I fired down the hallway. One of the kidnappers had taken up a position to the left where he was out of Miguel's line of fire. Fortunately, he was right in mine. I hit him three times in the center of mass. By my calculation, three kidnappers were dead, maybe more depending on whether Miguel had hit more. The odds were improving.

I couldn't see Miguel, but I immediately heard his AK chatter. I heard Miguel yell, "Send them!"

I told Ahmed, "Go on my signal and look for Miguel."

He nodded that he understood. I started firing and motioned for him to go. He disappeared into the kitchen with Miguel.

I did the same for Bashir.

Miguel yelled for me to go. As he started firing, I slithered on my stomach like an alligator in what the Army used to call the low crawl. In fact, it used to be a timed event in the annual Army physical fitness test. I could hear rounds snapping over my head that seemed to be coming from both directions. I came around the corner and found Miguel, Ahmed and Bashir huddled near the back door. Miguel said there was another dead one outside the back door.

It was about twenty yards to where the canvas was laid over the glass on the wall. Our improvised plan was to go back over the wall there and move to the pre-arranged rendezvous point.

I went out the door and tripped over the kidnapper Miguel had killed outside. I signaled for Ahmed and Bashir to wait for my signal and then follow me one at a time. I reached the wall. I could hear firing inside the house. I signaled Ahmed to come. He dashed to my location, and I boosted him over the wall. I didn't realize that Bashir had followed Ahmed without waiting for my signal. Just as Ahmed went over the wall, I started receiving fire from another outside corner of the house. I fell to a prone aiming position and fired shots. The kidnapper was shooting around the corner without looking or exposing himself to my fire. One of the rounds hit Bashir and he fell about five yards from me. I crawled over to him. The bullet had hit him in the right arm and knocked him down, but it was not life-threatening. I ripped off part of my shirt and wrapped the wound enough to stop the bleeding.

I turned around and Miguel was next to me. He grabbed Bashir and literally threw him up and over the wall. I made a stirrup for Miguel and in a flash, he was on top of the wall. He fired three short bursts and reached down to help me scale the wall. Five seconds later, we were all together on the other side. We quickly moved behind the house next door. Ten minutes later we arrived at the rendezvous point where the security team was waiting. The team had managed to bring Ahmed's car back to the rendezvous point as well. We stopped at a hospital on the outskirts of Tyre where they treated Bashir. They didn't ask what happened. It was midnight when we pulled into the Hilton in Beirut. We agreed to meet for breakfast to determine what to do next. Bashir stayed with me. Ahmed went home. But where the hell was Amir?

Chapter 47

Bashir was petrified that the terrorists would find him again. Fortunately, his wife and family were visiting relatives in Dubai. He called and told them to remain there and under no circumstances were they to return to Lebanon. We spend several hours talking about what had happened to him. He said, "One of the men came to my home claiming to have a special message from my brother, Amir. When I opened the gate, six more men burst into the house. They told me that I was being held to be sure that Amir did what he was told."

Bashir said that he had been kept bound and locked in the room where he was rescued. They fed him twice a day and allowed him to shower once in the past ten days. He had no idea how long they intended to hold him. He thought they might kill him in the end, since they made no effort conceal their identity. When asked if he had any idea where Amir might be, he said he thought he was still at his home in Texas.

We all met for breakfast at eight o'clock. Major Williamson joined Ahmed, Bashir, Miguel and me. We had agreed before Williamson arrived that we would not share the details of the rescue, especially the number of terrorists killed. We didn't want to create issues with local authorities.

I kept reminding myself that, despite all the death and drama, I still had not fulfilled my mission of finding Amir. In fact, I felt like I was further away from finding him than at any point since he had disappeared.

We discussed our options, which were few. We could go back to Tyre and try to find and interrogate one of the kidnappers or uncover evidence that could lead us to Amir. Nobody thought that was a good idea, since it was likely that the surviving kidnappers had left the area. We could call the search off, go home and hope that Amir would be released and come back to his family. The last option was to look to Major Williamson to see if he could provide some intelligence help from the U.S. Embassy here in Beirut. He responded, "I'll check with the FBI and Agency folks to see if they have anything they are willing to share with you guys."

We decided to stay at least one more day. I called Karen. She answered immediately. I said, "Hi Karen, it's John. How are you and Thomas?"

She replied, "Oh, John. It's so good to hear your voice. Thomas and I are fine. I've heard nothing from Amir. Do you think he is still alive?"

I said, "I think so. I thought we would find him in Tyre, but it turned out that the bad guys had kidnapped Bashir instead. We had a bit of a scrap, but we were able to rescue Bashir. He has a visa for the U.S., so we are going to bring him back with us."

She said, "That is fantastic news about Bashir. I like him very much."

I said, "I'm still hopeful that we can find Amir. Do you want us to stay longer?"

She responded, "If you can do it safely, please stay as long as there is still a chance to find Amir in Lebanon."

"Okay, we will stay at least a few more days and I will call you with updates every day."

Next, I called Captain Fortis in Houston. He answered promptly. I said, "Sorry to interrupt your golf game."

He said, "Yeah, asshole. Your damn call just caused me to miss a putt on eighteen. It will probably cost me first place here at the Shell Open. What the fuck do you want?"

I said, "Gee, I'm so sorry. Well, there is always next year."

I briefed him on the situation, including a blow-by-blow account of what had happened in Tyre. He said, "John, you are in a bad place. We Marines have bad memories of Beirut. If anything, the place has gotten worse. Watch your ass. I'm dead serious. As for what is going on here, the FBI has not provided HPD with any more information."

I hung up and pondered Fortis's comments. He was referring to the truck bomb that killed 220 Marines and twenty-one other American servicemen at their barracks at the airport. Fifty-four French paratroopers were also killed in a separate truck bombing on the same day. Fortis was right about Lebanon.

When all else fails, go to the gym. We agreed to reconvene for dinner at the hotel. Miguel and I went to the fitness center. It was equipped with a full array of machines and weights. We spent two hours on the weights.

Miguel is in great shape. I would hate to tangle with him in a fight to the death. We are both black belts in the Korean martial art of Hapkido. It is a true offensive fighting art, not to be confused with its Japanese cousin Aikido. During our final spar, our instructor, Master Pham, had to separate us and tell us to "just calm down." Miguel and I often laugh about what happened.

Miguel won the bench press with 275 pounds and ten reps. I was able to best him with twenty-five overhand pull-ups. We finished up with a three-mile run on the treadmills in nineteen minutes. I'm not a big fan of running on treadmills because of the boredom factor. I much prefer to run with my buddy, Pal, outside in the fresh air and among good-looking women.

Bashir chose to catch up on his sleep rather than work out. I couldn't blame him. We just finished our workout when something totally unexpected occurred.

Chapter 48

Miguel and I were walking out of the fitness center when I glanced at several attractive women on the stair stepper machines. I couldn't believe my eyes. There she was. I was certain I was looking at the dark-haired woman. After we left the center I said, "Miguelito, that's her. It's the dark-haired woman."

"Are you sure, Ranger? Could this be wishful thinking?"

I said, "I'm positive, no doubt."

We decided that we could not let her get away from us again. I called Ahmed and told him that we needed him at the hotel now and for as long as it took. He said that he was on the way. We decided that Miguel was the best person to follow her in the unlikely event that she recognized me from my previous visit to Beirut. I went back to the room. Miguel went back into the gym.

I took a quick shower, dressed, checked the weapons and walked back to the fitness center. Miguel was working out on the crunch machine. The dark-haired woman was still on the stair stepper. Five minutes later, she finished and walked out of the fitness center. Miguel stepped into the elevator after her. She had already pressed the button for the fifth floor.

Miguel asked casually, "Did you have a good workout?"

She responded in perfect English, "Yes, I definitely needed it. What about you?"

As the elevator stopped on the fifth floor, Miguel said, "Me too. Have a good day."

She exited the elevator and turned left. She stopped at room 516; Miguel kept on walking past her to the last room on the right and stopped. He acted like he was looking for his key card. When she entered her room, he walked down the back stairs to avoid walking past her room in case she was watching through the peephole in the door.

We all met in the restaurant to bring everyone up to date and plan our next move. Ahmed said that the manager of the hotel was his wife's uncle, and he would find out who was registered in room 516. I offered him $100, but Ahmed said that he wouldn't need anything but his good looks.

Ten minutes later, Ahmed was back with a big smile on his face. He laid down a Xerox copy of the dark-haired woman's American passport. He said, "Her name is Maria Ramirez, and her passport says she was born in Galveston, Texas."

I said, "Great job, Ahmed."

Ahmed beamed and said, "I also checked the registration card. She registered with an address in Brownsville, Texas. Does that help?"

Miguel said, "Sure does. That damn place comes up every time we turn around."

I called Major Williamson and passed on the information regarding Maria Ramirez. He said he would be over right away to pick up a copy of the passport. I also called Captain Fortis, Special Agent Roberts and Chief Rodriguez. Miguel went to the business center and made a copy of the passport for Williamson.

Miguel said, "I want to go to Maria's room, force my way in and make her tell me where the hell we can find Amir."

I responded, "I think we should wait and follow her. I think there is a good chance she will lead us to Amir."

Miguel argued, "Yeah, maybe, but on the other hand we might lose her again and be back where we were with no idea how to find Amir."

At that moment, Maria walked into the restaurant. She looked around and saw Miguel. Miguel waived. She waived back. Great! Maria and Miguel were bonding. She sat down at a table near the rear of the restaurant. It was obvious that she was waiting to meet someone. I said to Miguel and Ahmed, "Is it too much to hope that that Amir will walk in?"

Miguel said, "I will be the first to buy him a beer. Then I will tie him up and personally carry his ass to the airport."

A few minutes later, a man walked in and went straight to her table. It was not Amir. Ahmed almost jumped under our table when he saw the man. He whispered, "That's him! That is the one that was in charge at the house when I was taken hostage. That's him!"

I said, "Just be cool. Ahmed. Don't do anything that might attract his attention. You're the last guy he expects to see here in the restaurant."

I kept myself between Ahmed and the table where Maria and the kidnapper were sitting. Fortunately, the man was totally engaged with Maria and was not looking toward our table. The man was very animated as he spoke to Maria. I assumed he was describing what had occurred the night before at the house in Tyre. I wished I could hear the whole conversation.

I told Ahmed to walk out and have the team ready to go in case the two left. He was able to leave with no indication that he had been recognized. I felt like our luck was beginning to change for the better.

Chapter 49

Miguel left an envelope with a copy of Maria's passport at the Concierge desk with Williamson's name on it in case we had to leave before the major arrived. As Miguel was returning to the table, the kidnapper and Maria left the restaurant. She went toward the elevator. The kidnapper went toward the lobby. I made a command decision to follow the kidnapper.

Ahmed and the security team in the Toyota were waiting when we followed the kidnapper out the main entrance. There was an SUV waiting for him at the door. As soon as the SUV turned onto the main street and was out of sight, we jumped into the car with Ahmed. Fortunately, there was enough traffic to mask our following the SUV. The route was identical to the one Ahmed, and I had taken before we were shot at during my first trip to Beirut. However, this time we had the benefit of the security team with us. I called Major Williamson, who said he was almost to the hotel. I told him we had just left, but there was an envelope at the concierge desk waiting for him. As usual, he advised us to be very careful.

Ahmed was in cell phone contact with the security team leader. We decided to switch places with the Toyota when we got near where we had been taken under fire earlier before.

Shortly after the switch, the SUV pulled into gated house. We continued on. There was no indication that the kidnapper was aware that they had been followed. We pulled into a small bakery a block from the house where we could see the gate. We sent Ahmed into the bakery to buy baklava for everyone. Then we waited.

An hour later, another car arrived at the house. The windows were dark, and the car pulled through the gate making it impossible to know who had arrived. We contemplated the options. Miguel said, "We could go with another raid similar to the one in Tyre. It worked once. It might just work again."

I said, "In this case, the situation is different. We were not trying to rescue someone we know is inside. We have no idea how any people are in the house."

Miguel said, "Good point. There are more people on the street as well. I changed my mind."

We decided to wait. If we were going to conduct a raid, it was probably best done after dark anyway.

We had the Toyota drive by the house once to see if there were any sentries posted on the roof. None were spotted. The only apparent security was a guard at the gate where both vehicles had entered. At nine o'clock it was already dark. We had made the decision to go over the wall much like we had done in Tyre. Just as we were about to initiate our plan, the SUV drove out of the gate.

It was time for plan B. We followed the SUV back toward the hotel. It pulled into a gas station on Charles De Gaulle Street. The driver got out and spoke to the attendant. We pulled in behind the SUV with the Toyota in front. At that moment, the kidnapper opened the back door and got out of the SUV and looked around. The driver of the Toyota was waiting for the attendant, and everything seemed normal.

Miguel and I looked at each other. We both knew this was the best time to act. We walked as if we were going into the store by the gas station, pistols at our sides until we were within three feet of the kidnapper. Like a lightning bolt, Miguel was on him and had him in a choke hold with the gun to his head. The driver started to reach for his pistol, but he saw that I had him in my sights. He froze. I motioned for him to get on the ground. He complied immediately. I picked up his pistol and motioned for him to get into driver's seat of the SUV as I got in the back seat behind him. Miguel already had the kidnapper in the back seat of the SUV, and we pulled out. The whole operation was over in less than a minute.

Chapter 50

Ahmed took the lead and had us drive to a secluded spot near the Exhibition Center on the north side of Beirut. When we stopped, Ahmed climbed into the front seat of the Toyota to act as translator in the interrogation of the kidnapper. Miguel sat on one side of him, and I was on the other side. We both had pistols aimed at his head. We started by asking his name and organization. He refused to respond. Miguel told Ahmed to tell him that he had better start responding or they would find his body here in the morning with no fingers or toes. Still there was no response. Then there was an exchange between the two in Arabic. Ahmed said, "He says he isn't going to tell us anything and that he knows that Americans are forbidden from torturing anyone, so this is, how do you say, a bluff."

Miguel said nothing but hit the kidnapper in the nose with the heel of his hand. His nose flattened with a crack and blood gushed down onto his shirt. He screamed and grabbed his nose. There was a look of amazement on his face.

I told Ahmed, "Tell him not to believe everything he hears."

Ahmed spoke to him, and he answered immediately. He said his name was Mohammed Sharif. He said he was part of a group that had pledged allegiance to ISIS. When asked where Amir was, he said he didn't know. As soon as Ahmed translated Mohammed's response, Miguel was on him again. This time he drove the heel of his hand into his solar plexus. Mohammed bent forward gasping for air. When he was able to speak again, he said that they were holding Amir to be sure he supported an operation they were planning in Mexico and the United States. Ahmed asked him if he was in the house that Mohammed had left before going to the gas station where we grabbed him. Mohammed said that he was being held in the basement of that house.

We spent the next two hours getting all the details of the house. Our plan was to use Mohammed's SUV to enter the compound, overpower the guards, grab Amir and then leave. Mohammed claimed there were only four guards there and by eleven o'clock two of them would probably be asleep. Piece of cake!

At one in the morning, we arrived at the house. Mohammed and his driver were in the front seat just as they had been when they left the house five hours earlier. Mohammed's hands were tied behind his back, as were his feet. This would not be apparent unless the light in the vehicle was turned on or the guard shined a flashlight into the vehicle. Miguel was crouched on the floor in the back seat behind Mohammed with a pistol pointed at the back of Mohammed's head. Ahmed, who insisted on going along, was in the rear of the SUV. His mission was to alert us if either the driver or Mohammed said something to the guard that compromised our plan. I was crouched behind the driver, ready to shoot him if he alerted the guard that opened the gate. The head of the security team was also in the back with Ahmed.

We pulled up to the gate as planned. It took almost a minute before the guard, who was probably dozing, opened the gate. We drove in without any dialogue with the gate guard. So far, so good. The house was dark except for a light in what we had been told was the kitchen. As soon as the SUV parked, Miguel and I went into action. Miguel gagged and blindfolded Mohammed. I pulled the driver into the back seat, gagged and bound him with duct tape. In less than a minute, both prisoners looked like mummies. We laid them beside the SUV and Ahmed got behind the wheel ready to make our exit. He was to sound the horn if something went wrong. Fortunately, the SUV was not visible from the gate guard's position. Our security man was positioned to watch the mummies.

Chapter 51

As per our plan, Miguel was to take out the gate guard, then join me in the search for Amir in the house. Miguel sprinted to the wall and moved along it toward the guard shack. I went to the house. Everything was proceeding according to plan. Actually, it was better than the plan since we had no dialogue with the gate guard.

I looked into the kitchen through the window in the door. There was a bearded man at the table watching TV and drinking what looked like tea. There was an AK on the table in front of him. I tried the door quietly. It was not locked. Unfortunately, it was impossible to enter the room without being observed by the bearded man. I didn't want to lose the element of surprise with gunfire if at all possible. I slung the AK on my back and planned to only use the pistol. I could feel my adrenaline pumping as I burst into the room.

As soon as I entered the room, the bearded man reached for the AK. I had my pistol pointed at him and signaled for him to move away from the table. Instead, he grabbed the AK. I fired a double tap. Two rounds went into his head just above his nose.

He was dead before he hit the floor. The two shots definitely meant we had lost the element of surprise. Miguel came into the kitchen behind me and said, "Way to go stealth fighter."

According to the plan, Miguel covered the stairs going up while I went into the basement to rescue Amir. This time I carried a tool to cut through the padlock I expected to find on the door where Mohammed had told me Amir was being held. There was no light in the basement. I flipped on my flashlight and went to the room. The door was closed, but there was no padlock on the door. I opened and searched the room with the light. It was empty. Was it possible that they had just moved him? Was it possible that Mohammed had lied?

As I started up the stairs, I heard two more shots. When I arrived at the top step, Miguel was there. At his feet was another man sprawled on the floor with two shots to head. I signaled to Miguel that Amir was not in the basement. We cleared the rest of the first floor. There was no one there. That left the second floor. Going up the stairs was dicey, but we knew it had to be done. We had come this far and hopefully we were close to the end.

Miguel covered me as I went up the stairs. As I reached the top, I signaled for him to join me. At that moment, we heard a single shot come from one of the rooms down the hallway to the left. I feared the worst. It is what every member of a hostage rescue team is afraid will happen. The kidnappers will assassinate the hostage before the rescue team can get there. We moved slowly toward the door near the end of the hall. We each covered the other's movement. Miguel was on one side of the door. I was on the other. I felt certain that there would be a gun battle as we entered. Just as I reached for the doorknob, the door swung open, and Amir appeared. He had an AK in his hand, but immediately put it on the floor when he saw us. There was a man who appeared to be dead on the floor just inside the door. Amir said, “Oh my God! This is a miracle. How did you find me? This is the happiest moment of my life.”

I checked for a pulse in the man’s neck and determined that he was in fact dead. There was a bullet hole in the back of his head. I said, “Stay here while we check the rest of the house.”

He responded, “I think it is safe, there was one of them that went downstairs and then I overpowered this one and shot him.”

Miguel and I checked each of the other rooms on the floor. They were all empty. We returned to where we had left Amir. I said, “Let’s go home.”

As I turned toward the door, heard the shot and felt a burning sensation on my neck. The next thing I heard was a burst from an AK. At the open door to the bathroom behind me lay the naked body of a woman with a pistol in her hand. Miguel yelled for us to get down. He checked her pulse and announced her dead. He cleared the bathroom and came out with a towel and wrapped it around my neck. Miguel said, “You’ll live. It didn’t hit an artery or anything serious. It will leave a cool scar. Probably will attract the women.”

I said, “Yeah, with my luck they will probably think I cut myself shaving.”

I took a good look at the dead woman. It was the dark-haired woman. All the pieces were beginning to fall in place.

We all went down the stairs. Ahmed had the SUV ready. I was feeling a little faint, but happy that it was almost over. I climbed into the front seat with Ahmed. Miguel and Amir were in the back seat. We drove out of the compound.

I had the feeling something wasn’t right. Why was the dark-haired woman naked? Why was there no exit wound if Amir had shot the man guarding him with an AK? The wound had the makings of a small caliber weapon like a .22 pistol. I said to Amir, “That was pretty slick of you to shoot the guard with his own AK.”

Chapter 52

I felt the barrel at the back of my head. Amir told Ahmed something in Arabic. Ahmed stopped the SUV. Amir told Miguel not to move or he would kill me immediately. Amir said, "That was my mistake, you figured it out, didn't you?

I said, "It was a ploy all along, wasn't it, Amir? You tricked Karen into thinking you were being coerced. You were the mastermind of the whole plan, weren't you?"

Amir said, "Very good. I'll bet Mohammed told you I was being held captive, didn't he? That was the story in case any of the team was compromised. Unfortunately, now I can't let any of you live. I have to return to my sleeper cell in Houston.

I said, "What about the plan to kidnap Thomas?"

Amir responded, "That was part of the ploy, but you ruined it."

I said, "You mean you were going to put your family through the fear and pain of having your own son kidnapped? What kind of a person are you?"

Who are you to judge me! Yes, I was going to put them through some discomfort, but there was no intent to harm Thomas. Besides, this struggle is much bigger than all of us. We are warriors of Islam. We are true followers of Mohammed and the Koran. You and your unclean, disgusting country is the enemy. You are the great Satan. Allah will reward us for what we are doing. We will enjoy a special place in paradise."

I felt that I had to keep Amir talking if we had any chance of survival. I knew he intended to kill us. I said, "If your motives are so pure, how can you team up with drug running thugs in Mexico?"

Amir laughed, "You Americans are so naïve. Perhaps naïve is the wrong word, maybe stupid is more accurate. I suspect that you were a soldier. Didn't they teach you that you had to know your enemy? You don't have a clue about your enemy. You think differently. For us, the end justifies the means. There is no sin in deceiving and lying to your infidel enemy. We will use those thugs as long as they serve our purpose. We will kill them later."

"Does this mean you would also sacrifice Karen and Thomas as part of this plan that you have?"

He replied, "Well, Karen is expendable. I think there is hope for Thomas, but he needs to devote his life to the cause of Islam like I have done."

The gunshot was deafening. I felt bits of skull and tissue on the back of my head. I turned and saw what was left of Amir's head. It had been blown apart from the rear.

There, smiling in the rear of the SUV was Saif, Ahmed's uncle. He said something in Arabic to Ahmed who translated it, "He said he was sorry for making such a mess. If you hadn't taken his pistol, it would have been cleaner. The AK was messy!"

Miguel said, "Tell him it was the best mess I've ever seen."

Ahmed translated it and Saif laughed. We all laughed.

We drove to the rendezvous point and linked up with the remaining security. We left the SUV there with Amir's body inside. Miguel and I got into Ahmed's car, and we pulled away. The security team fell in behind us. There was no traffic as we headed back to the hotel. The ride to the hotel was quiet.

Chapter 53

Dawn was breaking as we reached the hotel. The call for the Morning Prayer was heard throughout the city. I felt a genuine sense of relief to be back in my room. Miguel washed my neck and rinsed it with peroxide before applying a large bandage to it. I fell asleep almost immediately.

It was eleven o'clock when the hotel phone rang. It was Major Williamson asking what happened. We agreed to meet for lunch at noon in the hotel restaurant. I called Karen and told her that Amir was dead. I said I would give her the details when I returned to Houston the next day. I called Captain Fortis and told him the same.

Miguel and I had lunch with Williamson. Miguel didn't want to tell him what happened, but I decided to share the story with him after swearing him to silence. We agreed that there was no benefit to letting it be known that Amir was a traitor and a terrorist. Williamson said he would try to recover Amir's body based on an anonymous report.

We all assembled for dinner to celebrate. Ahmed brought all of the security team with him. Bashir was there as well. We drank a toast to Saif, who had literally saved our lives the night before. It was truly a gathering of warriors from different continents and different cultures. The affection that we felt for one another brought tears to my eyes.

The next morning Ahmed was there to carry us to the airport. He was escorted by Saif's security team. Saif said his guys didn't want anything to happen to us going to the airport.

When we arrived at the airport, there were hugs all around. I felt a special closeness to Ahmed who had not only saved my life, but also had become a true friend for life. He is a great person. I told him to give my best regards to his wife and son. He thanked me and promised to give them the message.

Miguel, Bashir and I boarded the flight to Doha. I felt another real sense of relief as the plane lifted off the runway in Beirut. We breezed through the Doha airport and boarded the Qatar Airlines flight to Houston.

The beautiful flight attendant asked me what happened to my neck. It caught me totally by surprise. I stuttered and said, "I ran into a door." I heard Miguel moan. When I looked at him, he rolled his eyes and said, "Ranger, you're pathetic."

When she left, I asked Miguel, "What would you have said?"

"The fact that you have to ask makes you pathetic. I would have whispered in her ear that I was on a secret mission. I'll meet you in the galley in five minutes and tell you all about it."

Maybe I was imagining it, but from then on she seemed to look at me like I was a dork. I wanted to tell her, "I lied. I didn't really run into a door. I was on this secret mission." Unfortunately, I never got the chance. Every time she came close, Miguel chuckled. I reminded myself to punch him out when we got back to Houston.

We landed in Houston just after midday. The Custom agent checked my passport and said, "Welcome home, sir."

I responded, "Thanks, you have no idea."

Chapter 54

I waited for Bashir to clear customs. I had promised to drive him to his cousin's house when we arrived in Houston. After about sixty minutes, he came out. He said, "That was quite an ordeal. They took me into a separate room and asked me a million questions."

I said, "Your life is going to change for the better. What do you plan to do about your family?"

He said, "I really want to find a way to bring them to the States. I can't let them go back to our home in Lebanon."

We walked to the parking garage. I had to think twice about where I had parked my truck-a lot had happened since I left it. We loaded up and drove to the cashier stand. I always felt good about living in Texas every time I left the airport. There was no charge for parking when they saw the Purple Heart plate on my truck. The cashier said, "Thank you for your service, sir."

After dropping Bashir off at Habib's house, I drove home. As soon as I parked in the driveway, Mary Fitzgerald and Pal came out the door. Pal was dancing in circles when I got out. Mary gave me a bear hug. What a homecoming!

Mary said, "I'm preparing your favorite dinner – turkey, dressing with cranberry sauce, mashed potatoes and lots of gravy."

"Mary, I am in heaven!" Fortunately, I never got tired of turkey.

She said, "I want to hear all about your trip. I hope you took lots of pictures over there."

"Sorry, no pictures. But I made some new friends. I will be back in a couple of hours. I have to brief my client on what had happened.

Pal was rolling around at my feet trying to get my attention. I dropped to my knees and rub his belly. Now he was in heaven too. I motioned for him to get in the truck. He was there in a flash. As we drove off, Pal positioned himself in the backseat with his paws on the center console and insisted on licking my ear. Definitely man's best friend!

I called Karen to tell her I was coming over to her house. She said she was waiting for me. I told her it would be best if we met without Thomas. She agreed. When I pulled into her driveway, Karen was standing in the door. When we went into the house, she broke down. I held her and told her how sorry I was about Amir. I told her what had happened. I left nothing out. She listened without saying a word. When I finished, she said that she wasn't totally surprised. She said that she knew something wasn't right with Amir, but she would never have thought he was part of a terrorist cell.

Her comments seemed reminiscent of those of others who had been close to terrorists in sleeper cells hiding among us. There were always signs that should have alerted us to their presence and their intentions.

I said, "Listen, Karen, I intend to say nothing about what happened with Amir. There is no reason for Thomas to know the truth about his father unless you decide to tell him. I have Bashir's word that he will keep the secret as well."

She said, "Thank you so much, John. I can never repay you for all you have done. You and Miguel are my heroes. You both could have been killed. And please give me your bill right away and double it so that Miguel knows how much I appreciate what you both have done for Thomas and me."

I said, "Karen, you are my heroine. If you hadn't taken the initiative to come and see me when all of this started with Amir, the course of events could have been very different. A lot of innocent people could be dead right now. There is no doubt these terrorists had plans to bring down airliners. We could have had another 9/11."

I kissed Karen on the cheek, shook hands with Thomas, who had come out of his room as I was leaving, and I climbed back in my truck.

On the way home, I thought about all that had happened. It was a mental version of what we referred to in the Army as an after-action review. It was hard to imagine how we could have had a better outcome. However, we came very close to a real crisis. That success was a combination of good work mixed with no small amount of good luck. Had young Thomas not remembered that his dad was a fan of Rory McIlroy, we may never have even known that Amir was going to Lebanon. Had Miguel and I not been watching the apartment complex of the dark-haired woman, the white Mercedes laden down with missiles and other weapons might have never been intercepted. There were several points where I might have been able to find the terrorists faster. If I had gone to Amir's room in Beirut instead of alerting him by calling his room and leaving a message, I might have short-circuited their plan. If I had been able to capture one of the guys trying to kidnap Thomas or that followed me to Zippy's, maybe we could have stopped the plot sooner.

I knew I was over thinking much of what happened. Hindsight was always twenty-twenty. I thought about the really good people that had helped. Miguel was a superstar. I would not have survived the ordeal in Mexico or Lebanon without him. I was certain of that. Ahmed also came to mind. What a great person! He also saved my life. He showed extraordinary bravery at every turn. Those who referred to all Arabs and Muslims in negative terms should meet wonderful people like Ahmed and his family.

As I approached my apartment and parked the truck, I decided that all in all it was a pretty damn good operation. Before I got out, I made one more call. It was to Barbara. Life is good.

ABOUT THE AUTHOR

James Steele is a strong leader, a successful senior business executive, athlete and personal trainer, author, lecturer, and an expert in the areas of foreign policy, security and counterterrorism. He has worked extensively in some of the most interesting and dangerous places on the planet, including Iraq, Afghanistan, Pakistan, Mexico, Central America, Southeast Asia, and West Africa. His success in business is a matter of record having developed, financed, constructed, and operated energy projects valued in excess of $4 billion. His insights into security, unconventional warfare, insurgencies, counterterrorism, and law enforcement are based on extensive personal experience. He also is a personal trainer, certified by the American College of Sports Medicine. His acclaimed book, Move to the Sound of the Guns, is a dynamic account of experiences as a combat leader.

Steele is the founder and owner of JS Steele Enterprises, LLC, a Texas-based private security firm specializing in guard services, personal protection, security consulting and private investigations. He previously served as Managing Director of Focus Equities, a Canadian company headquartered in Victoria, British Columbia, with large land and infrastructure projects in western Canada.

In May 2013, Steele returned from Geneva, Switzerland, where he served as the CEO of Buchanan Renewables BV, an energy company engaged in power generation and supply of biomass from Liberia, West Africa, to major utilities in Europe. He was invited to lecture at the Harvard Kennedy School on his unique experiences in Africa. Prior to that, at the behest of the President of the U.S. Government's Overseas Private Investment Corporation, he worked in Afghanistan and the FATA region of Pakistan to advance economic development efforts that complemented U.S. policy objectives. Steele was also an owner of JD International, a private investigation and security firm based in Houston, Texas. In addition to private security work in Texas, at the request of the Governor of Sonora, Mexico, he assisted in the reorganization of the state police forces to deal with the mounting danger presented by drug cartels and organized crime in border areas. He became the principal interface between the state police of Sonora and the US Border Patrol. The SWAT team he trained made what was reported to be the largest drug seizure by a state police entity in Mexican history at the time. The same team was highly successful in a major battle against a Zeta force in the Mexican state of Sonora.

Steele served nearly three years in Iraq, working in the most conflicted areas of the country, including Baghdad, Mosul, Fallujah, Ramadi, Tikrit, Samarra, Tal Afar, Karbala and Najaf. From May 2003 until assuming the position of Senior Counselor to Ambassador Bremer for Iraqi security forces in November 2003, He was the senior police advisor with the Iraqi police SWAT unit in Baghdad. He headed the advisory team that organized, trained, and operated with this special unit. Steele led the unit on a series of highly successful operations that netted former high-ranking members of the Saddam regime as well as numerous other criminal and terrorist elements. During one such operation, despite intense fire, his team successful overpowered the terrorists and rescued two hostages that had been kidnapped, brutally beaten, and tortured by their captors. He participated in the raid that resulted in the capture of Saddam's former Minister of Interior, General Mohammed Zimam Abdul Al-Razzaq, the four of spades with a bounty of $1 million on his head. In April 2004, prior to the Marine offensive in Fallujah, Steele led a small group of

Iraqi police on an undercover operation into the city to assist in the recovery of the remains of the Blackwater contractors that had been ambushed and killed there, determine exactly what had occurred and assess the enemy situation. Because of an increasing threat throughout the country, Jim also assumed responsibility for the security of Iraq's most senior government officials, the members of the Governing Council. In the execution of this mission, he organized and supervised the training and equipping of over 300 members of the personal security details for members of the Iraqi Governing Council and key ministries. The success of this mission was repeatedly demonstrated by the superb performance of these protective security details under fire. In November 2004, the Iraqi commando unit that he was embedded with came under attack by a large insurgent force in Mosul. his actions during the battle were instrumental in defeating the enemy and saving the lives of both Iraqi commandos and U.S. soldiers. For his actions, he was awarded the Special Forces Gold Medal by the Government of Iraq. During the Iraqi elections in January 2005, the Iraqi commandos with which Steele was operating were a key force in protecting the polling sites in Baghdad and pivotal in the overall success of the election process.

Steele's efforts in Iraq received substantial press coverage and favorable mention in U.S. Congressional testimony. During hearings by the Senate and House Armed Services Committees, the Deputy Secretary of Defense described Steele as having "incredible bravery and also incredible expertise about police forces in third world countries." He characterized his work with the Iraqi police as "heroic." In December 2004, Secretary Rumsfeld presented Steele with the Department of Defense Medal of Valor for his actions under fire and the Distinguished Public Service Medal for his extraordinary service in Iraq. In an article in The New York Times Magazine, he was described, as "one of the United States military's top experts on counterinsurgency."

Steele retired from the U.S. Army after 24 years of service. He was consistently promoted ahead of his peers culminating in his selection for promotion to brigadier general, the youngest officer of his branch to be selected at that time. His promotion was pending Senate confirmation when he was recruited by Enron in 1991. He served in a series of senior executive positions there culminating in his assignment as managing director responsible for Enron's development activities in Europe, Latin America, and Africa. In early 1995, Texas oilman and former U.S. Secretary of Commerce, Robert Mosbacher, asked Steele to leave Enron and together form a new independent power company. He became President and CEO of Mosbacher Power Group. In that capacity, he led the successful development, construction, and operation of power plants in Texas, New Jersey, Virginia, and the Czech Republic.

During his military career, Steele served in a series of leadership positions ranging from a recon platoon leader in Vietnam to the deputy commander of U.S. Army South in Panama. His regimental commander in Vietnam, General George Patton Jr., described Steele as "the best small unit combat leader he had witnessed during two wars." In November 1968, as a young lieutenant. Steele led a small recon patrol that came under fire from a large North Vietnamese force. During the ensuing battle, he was shot twice attempting to aid a fallen comrade. After being evacuated to Japan to recover, he returned to Vietnam to command another recon unit in combat.

Steele's U.S. Army experience in Latin America related to security and counterterrorism is also extraordinary. As a colonel, he commanded the U.S. Military Group in El Salvador during the height of the guerrilla war. In addition to administering one of the largest U.S. military assistance programs in the world, Steele's team was credited with training and equipping what was acknowledged to be the best counterterrorist force in the region. He was also instrumental in the rapid response and negotiations that resulted in the safe return of President Duarte's daughter after she was kidnapped by FMLN guerillas. Upon his departure, he was awarded the Gold Medal of El Salvador. During "Operation Just Cause" in Panama, with operational control of an Army Special Forces Group, U.S. Navy SEALs, military police and civilian police advisors, Steele was the primary military interface with the new government and responsible for establishing a new professional police force. During an attempted coup in 1990, rebels comprised of former members of Noriega's military attempted to take him and his small team of advisors hostage. After an all-night standoff, Steele led the force that thwarted the coup and captured the rebels. For his actions, Panamanian President Endara awarded him the nation's highest award granted to a foreigner, the Order of Vasco Nunez de Balboa.

Steele's military decorations include the Silver Star Medal for gallantry in combat, the Defense Distinguished Service Medal, four Legions of Merit, three Bronze Stars (two for heroism and one for service), the Purple Heart, and various other service and campaign medals. he earned the Combat Infantryman Badge, U.S. Army Ranger Tab, Senior Parachutist Badge, as well as the Salvadoran Parachutist Badge, Special Operations Badge and Aviator Wings. He repeatedly received the Distinguished Instructor Award at the JFK Special Warfare Center and the Institute for Military Assistance at Fort Bragg, NC where he taught Special Forces and officers being assigned as attaches and advisors worldwide. He is a licensed private security manager, commissioned armed security guard, private investigator, and personal protection officer in Texas. Jim holds an Airline Transport License from El Salvador and a United States FAA Commercial Pilot License with helicopter and multi-engine and jet aircraft ratings. He is a martial arts expert with a Black Belt in the Korean art of Hapkido. He has lectured under the auspices of Premiere Speakers Bureau. He also previously served on the Texas Governor's prestigious Emergency Action Commission.

Steele earned a Bachelor's degree in Business Administration from the University of Dayton and a Master's degree in

International Affairs from the University of Florida. He is a graduate with highest distinction from Naval War College, a special fellowship graduate from the Army War College, and a German language graduate from the Defense Language Institute. He is certified in law enforcement operations and was awarded an honorary doctorate by the International Institute for Counterterrorism. He speaks Spanish and conversational German.

Jim is an avid supporter of Texas A&M University. His father, son and daughter are graduates. He lives in Bryan, Texas.

www.ingramcontent.com/pod-product-compliance
Lightning Source LLC
LaVergne TN
LVHW012047160826
845678LV00014B/2733